HORSE BOY

TANYA LANDMAN

WALKER
BOOKS

First published 2020 by Walker Books Ltd
87 Vauxhall Walk, London SE11 5HJ

Text © 2020 Tanya Landman
Cover illustration © 2020 Tom Clohosy Cole
Map © 2020 Jensine Eckwall

The right of Tanya Landman to be identified as author of this
work has been asserted by her in accordance with the
Copyright, Designs and Patents Act 1988

This book has been typeset in ITC Leawood and Humana

Printed and bound by CPI Group (UK) Ltd, Croydon CR0 4YY

British Library Cataloguing in Publication Data:
a catalogue record for this book is available from the British Library

ISBN 978-1-4063-7758-3

www.walker.co.uk

MIX
Paper from
responsible sources
FSC® C020471

For Victoria

PART 1

BOY

JOURNEY

The Deer people had no need of a stone circle: the mountains marked the turning of the year more accurately than anything humankind could construct. When the sun rose behind the tallest peak, pointing a finger of light across the upland plateau directly into the mouth of the sacred cave, it was midwinter. No matter how dark the nights, how deep the biting cold, Rowan, clan sage, took comfort in knowing that from that morning on the days would grow longer, a few heartbeats at a time.

It was her habit to mark the waxing of each new moon on the fingers of one gnarled hand. Little by little the moon of trees' slumber (pricked into her thumb) gave way to the moon of swelling buds (first finger). The moon of furred willow then yielded to the moon of first leaf burst. By the time the next crescent sliver climbed into the night sky, she'd marked her smallest finger and the moon of fresh oak leaves had begun. Soon, very soon now, it would be time. Each dawn she watched the sun edge its way along the horizon. And then, when it rose in the trough between the two smallest crags, Rowan nodded at Ashe, Deer chief. He gave the command at once: his people must leave their settlement and begin the journey to the clan meet.

This was no hunting party moving swiftly over difficult terrain, covering a great distance in a short time. This was the entire clan, who could travel only as fast as the slowest amongst them. The very old, the very young, the injured and the infirm reduced the rest to a snail's pace. Their presence also forbade going by the most direct route through Bear clan land, for that meant crossing the river and it was all too easy to slip on mossy stones and drown in the raging torrent. Instead, the Deer people would traverse the plateau in the direction of the setting sun, then turn north and head into the mountains until they reached the shadowy pass that cut a path through the highest peaks. Only when they emerged from that could they turn towards the east. Then they would walk through hill and vale for one moon's passing until they reached the flat, fertile plain where the great stone circle stood.

Once Ashe had spoken, it took the clan little time to prepare. In anticipation of the annual pilgrimage, provisions and the poles and hides that would serve as shelters while they travelled had long since been packed. Now sleeping sacks were quickly rolled, babies were tied to their mothers' backs, toddlers lifted to their fathers' shoulders. There were as many families in the Deer clan as the fingers on both hands. When they were all assembled around their matriarchs, Rowan – wrapped in furs, necklaces of bone and bark draped around her neck, feathers braided into her hair – stepped from her hut.

Rowan – seer of what has been and what is to come; healer, whose gentle hands smoothed the coming of souls into the world and eased their passing from it; sage, senior and most revered elder of the clan – settled herself on a litter woven from branches. As Ashe's strongest men hoisted her to their shoulders, a great shout rang out and the Deer people began to move.

Rowan was ancient as the sacred mountain and as strong. It was not for weakness or frailty she was carried, but out of respect to both her and the Goddess she served, for the clan meet was a sacred as well as a social occasion.

Oak, the chief's son, a boy poised on the brink of manhood, was brimful of energy and unable to contain his excitement. He strode ahead, then ran back, covering once, twice, many times the distance of the rest. His sleeping bundle bumped against his spine and the waist pouch banged so hard against his hip it would bruise him before the first morning was out.

"Calm down," said his sister Willow, laughing. "You're worse than Fang."

Oak and Willow looked at the dog that was racing in giddy circles around their father. Fang was full-grown now, leggy, deep-chested, with a growl as fearsome as a wolf's, but still with the mind and heart of an idiot pup.

The rest of the dogs kept their distance, hanging back more than a stone's throw behind the slowest of the clan. Smaller than wolves and darker of coat, they were feral thieves who would steal meat, snatch bones, grab anything edible if an opportunity presented itself. "Ravens without wings," Willow called them. "Pests. Scavengers too lazy to hunt for themselves." Most of the clan thought them a nuisance. It was only Ashe's fascination with the animals that kept the Deer people from driving the pack away.

Oak had made this same journey to the sacred

plain every summer of his life but the excitement never dimmed. To leave the mountains that hemmed them in, to become nomads like the other clans and walk for the waxing and waning of one whole moon to the stone temple, to see different peoples, hear different voices – he couldn't wait! Anticipation of future festivities gave that first day an air of joyful celebration. The elders laughed and speculated on what Ashe and Roc, the Bear clan chief, would disagree about this time. The building of huts? The planting of seeds? There was bound to be something. Unmarried men and women whispered behind their hands about what matches might be made – or broken. Children ran between them, racing, playing, bursting with the sheer joy of being alive and on the move.

Before long Oak fell into step between his friends – Yew, son of Thorn, and Lark, daughter of Apple. The three of them had been born the same summer. As babies they'd lain side by side under the trees staring up at the sky through dancing leaves. As toddlers they'd learned to walk together, tottering between the shelters hand in hand. Their first words had been spoken not to their mothers, but to each other.

Oak, his head full of the games and contests that lay ahead, wondered aloud who would win the most races this year.

Yew, ever the optimist, was certain it would be him. "It has to be my turn," he said. His short curls bounced as he walked. He'd got entangled in a gorse bush when they'd been playing the stalking game a couple of moons ago. Oak and Lark had been forced to cut him free with their flint knives, chopping off the locks that until then had reached halfway down his back. Deer clan only ever cut their hair in times of grief, so Yew's mother had fainted clean away when she'd seen him, thinking some deadly accident had occurred. They'd been in such trouble! And Yew's hair – sulking at being cut for such a trivial reason, Oak supposed – had so far refused to grow longer than the length of his thumb.

Yew slapped his thighs. "My legs have got longer over the winter, I'm sure."

Oak suppressed a smile. Yew's legs hadn't grown any more than his shorn hair but he never allowed reality to dent his enthusiasm.

"I can outrun you both now, easy." Yew grinned.

Lark raised an eyebrow. She'd shot up this last year and now stood a head taller than both boys. Slender as a reed, legs long as a heron's, she teased her hair out with a bone comb so it billowed in a cloud around her face. When the sun shone through it – as it did now – she had the look of a human dandelion.

"You may be a *little* taller than you were," she said, "but you're still too broad for speed. I'm the fastest."

"Never!" protested Oak. The other two were joking, but he was in earnest. "I'm the best, and you both know it."

"Prove it!"

"I intend to."

Jostling, punching each other's arms and play-fighting, the three expended so much energy that by the time the sun began to dip towards the horizon, Ashe's command to make camp came as a relief.

At the end of that first day, the clan stopped where it always did – high in the mountains beside a lake of such bright blue it looked as though a piece of sky had fallen to earth. The elders shared the necessary tasks, erecting hide shelters and setting cooking fires burning while the children ran and played.

After everyone had eaten their fill, the children settled down to sleep while the elders gathered around Ashe's fire. Oak, Yew and Lark, not yet elders but not quite children, walked down to the lake's edge together.

The water looked inviting enough but Oak knew that it was unpleasantly cold. Last year he'd played a trick on Yew and Lark, wading in until he was knee-deep, exclaiming over its delicious coolness when actually his feet had felt like blocks of ice.

"It's glorious!" he'd said as he waded back to the shore. Then he'd pointed to a rock that jutted over the deep water. "We could jump off that and have a swim. Race you!"

He'd sprinted along the shore towards it but been deliberately slow, stumbling over his own feet, letting the other two overtake him. When they'd jumped off, he'd stopped dead. He'd watched them leap in and then swim back to the shore shivering with cold while he'd stood warm and dry, laughing until the tears ran down his cheeks.

Oak had no intention of going in this year either, but Yew obviously remembered the prank as clearly as Oak did. "Go on in," his friend said with a grin. "Swim. I dare you."

Oak hesitated. But then Lark raised her hand to her mouth and behind it whispered loudly to Yew, "What was it that Rowan foretold at this boy's birth?"

In a mock whisper of his own Yew answered, "That the clan's fortunes would rise with him."

Lark shook her head. "No. I can't see it myself," she said. "I think our future chief is a coward!"

It was enough. Ripping off his tunic, Oak ran along the same rock he'd avoided last year and jumped into the deep water.

The impact of the cold was as savage and sudden as a fist in the face. It wasn't simply unpleasant; it was deadly. As the water closed over his head, Oak was seized with a wild panic. The lake had him in its grip. It wouldn't let him go ... it would drag him down ... crush him!

Thrashing wildly, he broke the surface, shrieking with relief as his lungs filled with air. Moments later he was standing, dripping and shivering on the shore.

Yew, doubled up with sniggers, could barely get the words out. "You baby! What a noise!"

"Did the poor little boy get wet?" Lark was giggling helplessly. "Just as well the snows have melted. That yelp would have caused an avalanche!"

Oak was chilled to the marrow. "It's not funny," he wanted to say, but his teeth were chattering too hard. The joy of the day had vanished and tears of fury now sprung to his eyes. How dare they laugh? He was the chief's son – they shouldn't mock him like this; they had no right! Suddenly tired of his friends' company, Oak pushed between the pair, and leaving them at the water's edge went to join his sister by the fire.

Willow took one look at him and wrapped her own cloak about his shoulders, then handed him her vessel of broth. She said not a word: Rowan was speaking, and when the sage opened her mouth the words of the Goddess poured forth. After Oak had finished drinking, Willow took his hands in hers to warm them, but it took a long time for him to stop shivering.

Ashe and the elders were listening to Rowan attentively, heads cocked to one side, frowns creasing their foreheads. Oak knew that a boy of his age would not normally be allowed at such a meeting. He was tolerated only because he was the chief's son, though why anyone would choose to attend such a dull gathering was beyond him! He paid little attention until Rowan suddenly mentioned the lake from which he'd just emerged.

"The water is very low," she said. "I'd hoped the drought was confined to our plateau, but it seems the rains have not fallen here, either."

Oh, thought Oak. Was that why the lake water was even colder than he'd recalled? The warm spring rains would have taken the edge off, he supposed, the way dropping hot stones into a cooking skin heated the liquid inside. He'd tell Yew and Lark he'd had good reason to shriek – if they ever stopped sniggering long enough.

He was dimly aware that the winter had been unusually dry but it hadn't bothered him: he had enjoyed not having to wade through endless mud. Yet here was Rowan, telling the elders that without rain the grass could not grow. It was why the deer herds hadn't yet returned to their territory, she declared. He looked at the worried faces gathered around the fire: elders, sucking their teeth, looking at the night sky, frowning.

"And the cause?" Ashe said softly. "There must be a reason."

"The Goddess holds back the clouds," Rowan said. "Something has offended our Mother Earth. She has not yet shown me what."

The elders muttered uneasily. Whispers passed from mouth to mouth about what – or who – had upset the Goddess on whom all their lives depended. Oak shivered, this time not simply with cold. Surely they were worrying over nothing? The Goddess had been as generous the year before as she always had been. The hunters had found prey for moon after moon until the cold had driven the herds away. The elders of the clan had dried meat in strips and pounded it into mash to be stored in the caves: Oak had sat and watched vessel after vessel being stashed away. The children had helped with gathering nuts and seeds and berries, and the corn Ashe planted in the spring had grown well and been harvested. There was plenty of food cached – enough to feed the clan for a long time to come. And besides all that, there were still fish in the river and birds in the sky. Hares and goats still ran in the mountains – the Deer people would not starve. And the Goddess could not withhold the rains for ever!

Oak, suddenly irritated by the elders' frowns and their anxious conversation, got up. Leaving Willow's side, he entered his family's shelter, wriggled into his sleeping sack and settled down for the night.

STONE TEMPLE

The following dawn Oak's mood lifted, his anger at Lark and Yew melting away like the early mist. They were his friends, weren't they? And didn't they love making this journey? Didn't they all want to have some fun?

Perhaps sensing that they'd pushed him too far, Lark and Yew said nothing more about Oak's brief lake swim. For the length of that morning the three of them laughed and joked as they had the day before. But by the time the sun was at its highest and the clan had stopped to rest and eat, Oak could ignore it no longer: Rowan's words from the evening before hung over the clan like a dark cloud. Brows were still furrowed, mouths were still downturned. Mothers were clutching their infants a little too tightly.

As Oak's eyes scanned the elders' faces, Lark followed his gaze.

"What's wrong?" she asked.

"Nothing!" said Oak.

"It doesn't look like nothing. What were the elders talking about last night?"

"It wasn't anything important," he snapped. "They're all being ridiculous."

Before Lark could ask him anything else, Oak moved away.

Yet no matter how fast he walked in the days that followed, no matter how hard he tried, Oak couldn't escape the truth. When they emerged from the mountain pass and entered the foothills, it was evident to every member of the clan that the land was unrelentingly parched. The grass was brittle and yellow, not green and fresh-sprung. The earth beneath it was baked so hard it was cracked in places. The valley rivers they relied on for drinking water were reduced to streams, the air around them hazed with swarms of flies. As feet grew blistered and limbs started to ache, everyone was increasingly ill-tempered. Elders were sullen and serious, children – catching their parents' mood – peevish and irritable. Lark and Yew grated against Oak, play-fights turning into real ones. Even Willow – who could always be relied on to be cheerful company – was peculiarly quiet and withdrawn.

"The elders are worrying for nothing, aren't they?" he asked her one evening. "We've plenty of food stored!"

He was hoping for reassurance, but Willow gave him none. She shook her head and said, "What do you think we have been living on this last winter? Our supplies are almost exhausted and we have so many mouths to feed. If the deer do not return after the clan meet..."

She turned away, leaving her sentence hanging. Her mind seemed to drift off – there was a distant look in her eyes. Oak had the strange, uneasy feeling that it wasn't simply the lack of rain that occupied her thoughts. There was something else, some secret she was hugging to her chest. He pestered her to talk to him, trying to irritate her into conversation, but she remained quietly distracted.

By midsummer's eve Oak was footsore, hungry and sick to death of every single member of the Deer clan.

But then at last came the glorious moment when they crested the final hill and Oak saw the vast plain spread out at his feet like a robe, the stone circle at the centre crawling with so many people it resembled an ants' nest that had been kicked.

Midsummer.

The clans gathered.

Days of feasting and fun lay ahead. Surely those furrowed brows would smooth themselves now?

Oak drew in a deep breath, inhaling the faint scents of cooking fires, of meat and mead, of sweat and excitement. Down there, peculiarly pale-skinned traders from distant lands would be moving through the camp selling strange goods and telling even stranger stories. Old men and women would gather and share their memories of times gone by. Young ones would laugh and flirt and look to the future.

At this distance he could hear nothing, but he could imagine the hum of conversation, the shouts of laughter, elders greeting friends and relatives they hadn't seen for twelve moons and his heart soared. If a man married outside his own clan, it was the custom for him to join his wife's people, unless he was a chief. When Ashe had married Oak's mother, she'd left her Fox clan for the Deers. Her sister, Oak's Fox aunt, would soon be squeezing Willow to her bosom. Then she'd cup Oak's face in both hands and her eyes would fill with tears as they did every year. His aunt would lament again about how his mother had died giving life to him, and he'd stand there wondering how to reply. Then his Fox uncle would break the awkward silence by pinching Oak's cheek, ruffling his hair and telling him how much he'd grown. After that Oak would be free to run off with his cousins – Celandine, his own age, Hawk, a year younger. He couldn't wait to see them.

Just then the sound of horns reached Oak's ears. Five short blasts. One long one, announcing that the sacred ritual was about to begin. A sudden panic swept through his clan.

"The drought has slowed us down." Rowan looked at Oak's father. "We're barely in time!"

"Hurry!" barked the chief.

Already the sun was low in the sky. The other clans' sages had begun chanting, and somewhere out of sight the dancers would be preparing. The air throbbed with anticipation.

Down the slope they ran, across the plain, Rowan clinging to the sides of her litter to avoid being thrown out as her bearers sped towards the temple. The rest of the Deer people hurried towards the river to make camp between Bear and Fox clans as they did ever year.

The elders erected shelters, fumbling and clumsy in their haste. Oak heard few calls of greeting from the other clans, saw few welcoming smiles and no warm embraces. There was simply no time for such things: the Goddess must be properly honoured and the sun was sinking lower with each indrawn breath.

Oak was the only member of the clan to remain perfectly calm. The sacred rite was for the elders alone – he was free to do as he pleased. He was about to go and find his cousins when he felt his father's hand on his arm.

"You're not running off. Not this time."

Oak opened his mouth to protest but his father silenced him with a look. "You're a child no longer. You stand on the threshold of manhood. It's time for you to join me at the ritual."

Oak's heart sank. Not this year surely, he thought, nor even the next! He was supposed to have two more summers of freedom before duty crushed him. Had his father discussed this with Rowan? Had they agreed it between themselves, or was this Ashe's own decision? Oak supposed it was meant as some sort of honour, that he should have counted it a privilege, but the very thought made his skin crawl with boredom. He remembered some years back when he and Willow had crept to the edge of the stone circle and lain in the long grass, chests aching with the effort of containing their excited laughter. They'd watched it all in secret.

The ritual had started dramatically enough with masked dancers, magically sinister in the light of flaming torches, emerging from behind the stones. But then the prayers, the chanting, the slow movements and the invocations of the sages had gone on for ever! They had sent Oak to sleep long before the sunrise.

True, it had become more interesting at dawn. Willow had prodded her little brother awake and they'd watched a boar dragged forth and tied, squealing and terrified, between two stakes. Their own father had caved in its skull with his axe and slit its throat, letting its blood spill upon the earth. Its carcass was butchered by the sages, hunks of bone and flesh and guts set in the roaring fire to burn to ashes.

The boar's life had been sacrificed to feed the Goddess. Now Mother Earth would have the strength to keep the seasons turning, to hold the stars in the heavens, to roll sun and moon across the sky for another year.

Having seen one ceremony, Oak had no desire to watch another. But he could hardly tell his father that. Besides, Ashe had not finished talking. Every word fell like a boulder on Oak's back. He felt himself sinking into the same dismal mood as the rest of his clan.

"You are chief-in-waiting and there is something very wrong with the earth. We must discover what has offended the Goddess and I need your eyes and ears. There will be no playing at this clan meet. You must walk beside me at all times and pay close attention to all that is said. Absorb the wisdom of your elders. Listen when the chiefs speak. Worship with the sages when they pray. Respect them, but do not forget to think for yourself, too. Think, Oak. Think."

Respect the sages? A small sigh escaped Oak. He'd had a bellyful of Rowan's mystic mumbling on their journey. He'd barely been able to sleep at night because of her endless praying. And where had it got them? The drought still hadn't broken.

Ashe increased the tightness of his grip, forcing Oak to look into his eyes. He seemed to read his son's thoughts: he shook his head and said wearily, "You have so much to learn. Goddess! I hope I haven't left it too late."

CLAN MEET

And so, that midsummer night, Oak stood in the stone circle on one side of his chief, simmering with resentment. Willow wasn't here as far as he could see. Though his sister was old enough to be counted an elder, she seemed to have slipped away. Where was she? As for Yew and Lark – had they met up with Celandine and Hawk by now? What were they doing? Whatever it was, they'd be having more fun than him.

At Ashe's other side stood Fang. The chief had tamed the pup last year, and now the dog watched the ceremony through amber eyes, more interested and attentive than Oak could ever be.

The ceremony began at dusk. As the sun finally sank below the horizon, torches were lit. Then masked dancers came weaving between the stones – wearing skulls of deer, bison, boar. One, twice as tall as the others, bore the monstrously large skull of an aurochs, its horns as long as Oak's arms. When he'd watched that first time as a small child, he'd been enchanted – they'd seemed like wondrous spirits from another world. But now he was in no mood to be impressed. He could see only too clearly the human figures beneath. The aurochs dancer was not unnaturally tall, but simply one person sitting on the shoulders of another. Over there was Thorn, Yew's father, under a stag's skull – it was obvious from his lopsided gait. He'd been gored by a boar on a hunt years ago and the leg had never properly healed. And there was Apple, Lark's mother, wearing the smaller skull of a hind, trying to imitate its movements but failing miserably because what human could truly capture the light steps and the tense, twitching wariness of a deer? The dancers didn't look mystical, they looked ridiculous – grown people pretending to be something they weren't. Was this really supposed to please the Goddess?

They moved around each other, circling, swaying in time to a slow, steady rhythm, feet stirring up clouds of dust that caught in Oak's throat. What was he going to die of first? Choking? Or boredom? He was stifling another yawn when the drumming increased in tempo and volume and the chanting began as painted men and women sprang out from between the stones, spears in hands. They chased the masked dancers in a ritual enactment of a hunt, charging, retreating, swirling, the pace becoming more frenzied as the darkness thickened.

Once the hunters had triumphed over their prey, the sages began wailing prayers to the Goddess. There was Rowan, standing beside the heavily tattooed Bear clan sage, the palms of both raised to the stars.

They would keep it up until dawn, Oak knew. And he was supposed to stand there wearing an expression of reverence like a mask. Every muscle ached and he could barely keep his eyes open. He had to bite the inside of his cheek to stop himself yawning.

Oak's attention slipped. His eyes wandered to the watchers gathered around the circle. There were as many clans as the fingers on both his hands and the chiefs stood flanked by elders. Their faces all had the same downturned mouths and furrowed brows that the Deer people had worn this last moon.

It didn't trouble Oak but it did annoy him. Elders were always fretting about something or other: too much sun, too little rain... In a moon's time it would be the other way around. They'd sit by the fire worrying about grey skies and floods and asking what had displeased the Goddess this time?

He was trapped while all his friends were having fun. The thought of them enjoying themselves without him chafed Oak's temper raw. Why was he here? It wasn't fair! The son or daughter of a clan leader didn't always inherit the title – it was a matter for sages and elders to decide when the time came. But Oak had been named chief-in-waiting at the moment of his birth. Rowan had been granted a vision that he'd been chosen by the Goddess herself. He'd always revelled in his status, but now for the first time it felt like an unwelcome burden. If this was what being a leader meant, then maybe he wasn't so keen on it after all.

The ritual was only the beginning. Days of mind-numbing, flesh-crawling tedium followed. There was endless talking, and all the time Ashe kept his son by his side, tethered with cords of duty that were strong as hide.

The talk was only ever of the drought and what had caused it. The chiefs agreed that something had displeased the Goddess and looked to the sages for an explanation. But despite their reverence, their worship, their sacrifices, the sages could not give one. They prayed, they lit fires and burned sacred herbs, but no visions came.

And so the chiefs thrashed around like blind men in the darkness, grasping for hints or clues that would tell them why the Goddess was unhappy.

Oak did not listen to much of it: his attention was almost always elsewhere. His ear was fine-tuned to the noise of the pack of children that roamed wild and free without him. He could hear their shouts and cheers when they raced or wrestled; their shrieks of laughter coming from the copse at the far side of the plain. He knew even without turning his head what was going on. There was a beech tree there with a branch that stuck out sideways, bending low to the ground before shooting skywards again. It was thick as a man's waist, yet supple as a whip of willow. Yew and Lark would be there with Oak's cousins and all the other clans' children, taking turns to sit astride while the rest pushed and pulled the branch this way and that, trying to dislodge the rider. Last summer they'd turned it into a competition, one clan against another. He'd been the Deers' champion. No matter how hard they'd tried, no one had been able to shake Oak off. He'd bested all of them. The boy from the Fox clan – what was his name? Rit? Rin? Rig? Something like that... He was a friend of Hawk's, anyway. He'd got close to winning, but Oak had beaten him. And then they'd wrestled and Oak had won again. It had felt so good!

But now, this summer, here he was, stuck with elders who chased each other in verbal circles, going endlessly round and round, the arguments on one person's lips contradicted by those on another's. It was so tedious that Oak did what he'd never imagined possible: he started counting down the days until it was time to leave.

At last – after the worst clan gathering of Oak's entire life – came the evening of the final feast. The next morning the clans would return, each to their own territory. For Oak, dawn could not come fast enough.

The sages had joined together at the temple for one last, desperate attempt to discover from the Goddess what had caused the drought and what could be done to appease her.

Oak and Willow had watched in previous years and laughed at the chiefs' behaviour. It never seemed to matter how bitterly their father disagreed with Roc, the Bear leader, during the clan meet: at the final feast any discord was drowned in mead. With every passing of the drinking horn, their protestations of eternal friendship grew louder and more lavish.

But not this year. This year the air between Ashe and Roc seemed cold as ice, despite the roaring fire. Oak felt its chill as he sat glumly beside his father watching the children slipping away one by one to play in the woods.

Willow herself had disappeared almost at the start of the proceedings saying she needed to relieve herself, but she hadn't come back. Was she ill? She hadn't looked it. He suspected it was an excuse, that was all. His sister was Goddess-alone-knew-where, doing Goddess-alone-knew-what with Goddess-alone-knew-who. He'd tried to point out her absence to their father but Ashe was too deep in thought to care what his daughter was doing.

The rest of the chiefs were as preoccupied as his father. There was no jovial talk this year, no laughter nor declarations of brotherly love. Even the flames seemed flat and subdued.

Ashe ate and drank less than usual and spoke barely a word. The mead horn went around and around and the elders slumped deeper into themselves.

After what seemed like a very long time, the sages finally finished their praying and joined the feast.

Eagerly, elders and chiefs sought answers in their faces, but the seers brought not a trace of hope or relief with them. Mouths were straight, grim lines, heads were shaken. The Goddess had clearly held her tongue despite their pleading.

Finally Ashe decided he'd had enough. When

Rowan passed him the mead horn one last time, he pushed it aside. "I'm away to sleep."

The old woman frowned. "There is only one mouthful left, my chief," she said. "It would offend the Goddess if you did not drink it."

Ashe grunted but swallowed obediently enough. Yet Oak's father had been right thinking he'd had enough. Only a few moments later, with the moon still high overhead, Ashe started to doze where he sat, Fang's head in his lap.

There was a bark from the edges of the camp and the dog pricked up its ears, sniffing the air. It seemed restless, perhaps wanting the company of its own kind for a while. Fang glanced at Ashe and sat up.

The cords of duty that bound both dog and son to Ashe's side seemed to slacken.

Fang hesitated, but Oak saw his chance and took it. Slowly, quietly, he got to his feet and, praying to the Goddess that his father wouldn't wake and call him back, went looking for his friends.

STALKING

Sprawled on the grass near the river, those who were halfway between the worlds of elders and children were having their own clan gathering. It didn't take Oak long to find his friends. He looked for Lark first and thought there was something wrong with his eyes, for there were not one but two girls with orbs of hair that glowed in the moonlight.

"Lark!" he called.

Both girls turned and he saw that only one of them was her. The other was his cousin Celandine. Lark waved the bone comb she held in her hand by way of greeting but then went back to what she was doing – teasing out Celandine's hair still further and then studding it with the same flowers she was wearing. He could tell from their chatter that they were dazed and giddy from laughter and lack of sleep.

He couldn't see his cousin Hawk. Perhaps he was in bed already. Where was Yew? Surely he'd still be up?

His eyes scanned the group. There he was! Deep in conversation with that lad from the Fox clan who'd come so close to beating Oak last year. What was he called? Rot? Rag? Rat? He still couldn't remember.

Oak called Yew's name as he headed towards the pair. He half expected his friend to get up, run over and greet him but Yew stayed where he was.

Oak squatted down on his haunches beside them.

"Oak," Yew said, grinning, "we've missed you! Riff's won everything without you to challenge him." He punched the Fox lad playfully on the arm.

Riff. That was it. The boy smiled briefly at Oak.

"You came very close to winning that last race," Riff said generously to Yew. "If only you hadn't tripped."

Lark called across the grass, "Are you sure you didn't bribe someone to put that stone there? Was it you, Celandine?"

The four of them laughed as if it was the funniest joke on Mother Earth. And then others chipped in.

"What about when you fell off that branch?"

"Flat on your face!"

"You looked so angry!"

"*I* looked angry? What about you when you slipped in the river?"

"You squealed like a boar!"

"And then when Hawk..."

Whatever Hawk had done was lost in a gale of giggles.

Oak felt thrown off balance. He'd thought they'd welcome him like a victorious hunter returning home, that they'd be hanging on his every word, or would at least show some sign of having felt his absence! Instead, he felt like an intruder. While he'd been stuck with his father, they'd formed their own clan – and he wasn't leader of it.

After what seemed like a very long time, the laughter faded and an awkward silence took its place.

"What about you?" Lark said eventually.

"What did the chiefs say about the drought?" asked Celandine.

Oak didn't like to admit that he'd barely listened. Even if he had, what could he say that wouldn't make his friends' eyes glaze over with boredom?

"Nothing much," he said. Another awkward pause stretched out. Oak stood up suddenly. "I'm going to get some sleep."

"Are you all right?" asked Riff.

"Tired, that's all," Oak replied shortly.

They all said goodnight to him kindly enough, but he hadn't gone far before he heard laughter at his back. Were they mocking him? No ... they were his friends. They wouldn't do that. But he felt hot and uncomfortable just the same.

He'd find Willow, he thought. His sister was always ready to listen to him; she always made him feel better. He returned to the camp, but she was nowhere to be found. Where in the name of the Goddess was she? Not amongst the old and infirm or the smallest children who lay sleeping in their family shelters. Not with the elders who had come away from the feast and now sat talking earnestly to one another. Who was she with? And why hadn't she told him what she was up to?

He didn't know what to do or where to go. He supposed he should rest, but he fizzed with irritation. He couldn't sleep, not yet.

He began to wander back towards where his father had dozed off under the stars. Perhaps he should rouse Ashe, persuade him back to the shelter?

He'd reached the copse when a movement in the shadows caught his eye. He froze; slowly turned his head. Someone was sitting on the bending beech branch. Something familiar in the figure's posture told him it was Willow but he didn't call her name because someone else was there too, someone he didn't recognize. A man. And there was something furtive about the pair that aroused Oak's curiosity.

The stalking game was Oak's favourite. One child was selected as prey, the others were the hunters. The prey would choose a vantage point to wait and watch while the hunters scattered and hid. Their challenge was to creep up without being seen and get near enough to hurl a small stone. If a hunter hit the prey before their name was shouted out, they were the winner. It was another thing he'd missed this clan meet. Until now.

He crept towards the tree, keeping low to the ground, pausing each time the pair's murmured conversation fell silent. They were sitting close together, heads tilted towards each other but not quite touching. Oak could feel a strange tension between the two of them, tight as a bowstring.

Was this the secret she'd hugged to her chest on the way here? Who was that man? It was no one Oak recognized. Not of their own clan, then. Fox? Bear? Raven? Wolf? Anything was possible. All Oak could see was his profile – a sharply pointed nose, like a beak, and a thick mass of hair.

Oak was nettled. His sister had never shown interest in a man before! And she knew the customs of the clans as well as he did. A woman of her age was usually free to choose her own husband, but Willow was the daughter of a chief. Both sage and elders would have to approve her choice before she could be handfasted. Yet here she was hiding from their eyes. Oak's sister was transgressing. Should he wake their father? Tell him?

No ... not yet.

Oak was the hunter, Willow the prey. He squatted on the ground, his palms flat on the grass. Beneath his knife hand he could feel the outline of a small stone. His fingers closed around it.

He couldn't resist. Taking aim, breathing out slowly, he hurled it towards the pair. He'd aimed squarely at Willow, but the moment it left Oak's hand, the young man leaned forwards as if to kiss her. The stone struck him hard. From his yelp and the way his hand went to his face, Oak guessed the missile had caught his cheek just below the eye.

The couple looked around wildly, Willow so startled that Oak couldn't help laughter escaping his lips.

"Oak!" Willow's angry cry was followed by a furious string of curses.

Oak turned tail and ran back to the shelter. Her words followed him but he didn't care. He'd won and that would do. For now.

He knew her secret. He could hold it in his hand like a weapon, use it at any time he chose.

FURY

Oak dreamed.

He was standing at the stone temple, not at his father's side but alone in the centre, tethered to the stakes with rope as if for sacrifice.

Dancers came from the shadows, spinning, twirling, circling him in a wild frenzy, then stopping, pulling off their masks. He looked from face to face. Yew, Lark, Celandine, Hawk, Riff – all his friends – surrounded him. They were laughing. Sneering. And then Willow stepped forward with an axe and raised it high above his head.

It fell, the blade biting deep, and he was screaming, howling like a wolf, a long, agonized cry of pain and betrayal. And then the sound wasn't coming from his own throat, but from that of another.

Oak jerked awake, hot, sweaty, gasping for breath, his heart and mind racing. He tried to calm himself, inhaling deeply, but he could still hear the sound of an animal, now baying for blood.

He crawled from his sleeping sack to the mouth of the shelter. In the moonlight he saw his father standing, face contorted with rage. Whether the noise had come from him or from the man Ashe held by the throat was impossible to say. Ashe's fingers were like bloodied claws, pressing into the man's windpipe, choking him. But the man, though torn and bleeding badly, fought back, suddenly smashing fist and knee so hard into Ashe's belly and groin that the Deer chief fell to the ground.

Befuddled with sleep, it took Oak a moment to recognize Roc. The Bear chief, fighting his *father*? Here? In the Deer camp? He must still be dreaming. It was impossible!

A crowd had gathered. Oak scanned their faces and saw his own shocked confusion reflected in their eyes. The whole of the plain where the stone circle stood was holy ground. Tests of strength and light-hearted wrestling contests were permitted, but serious conflict was utterly forbidden. Oak had never seen a man raise his hand against another in deadly earnest.

Ashe staggered to his feet. His hand went to his

knife. A collective gasp from the onlookers made him pause, and Oak was in no doubt that more blood would have been shed had not Rowan stepped in front of his father and pressed both hands to the chief's chest.

"No!" she said. "Do you forget where you are?"

"I do not!"

Ashe lowered his knife, but his fury did not abate. He spat in Roc's face.

And then – when Oak thought things could not get worse – came the dreadful, dreadful words: "Goddess, be my witness. We are brother clans no more. From this night on, every Bear is an enemy to the Deer people." Ashe held his knife at arm's length, pointing at the crowd, slowly turning full circle so all the watchers could hear him. "We do not set foot on their soil. And if any Bear enters our territory, it will be an act of trespass punishable by death. You, Roc –" Ashe jabbed towards the chief – "what you have done can never be forgiven. If ever you cross my path – whether it be on my land or that of any other clan – my knife will taste your blood. So help me, I'll slit your throat to the bone."

If Roc answered, Oak didn't hear. The commotion that followed Ashe's threat drowned out everything. Had his father taken leave of his senses? For one chief to threaten another was unheard of. And to do it here, at the sacred site! To give the Goddess such offence, it was beyond belief! Yet Oak had heard the words with his own ears.

And now his father was striding between the Deer clan shelters, rousing those who miraculously still slept, ordering his people to leave the clan meet. Now. At once. In the dark.

There were mutterings of dismay. Cries of alarmed confusion. Questions. All cut dead by Ashe's roar.

"Enough! We do not debate this! It is my order. We leave this place now. Anyone who disobeys will be outcast."

Outcast?

Trespass?

Punishable by death?

These were words from tales told around the fire, tales told to make children's eyes grow wide with fright, tales of the savage, wild times before the clans were brothers. The words had no place in the real, living world. Yet here they were. Uttered by his own father.

Sick with fear, Oak rolled his sleeping sack and bundled it onto his back. He tied his pouch to his waist, hands fumbling with the knots. Already his father was striding alone across the plain, a flaming torch in his hand. Was he abandoning their precious shelter? Should Oak pack it? He didn't know how! Where was Willow? He looked about him frantically. But everything – everyone – was a blur. Only his father's disappearing back was clear and in focus.

He must not be left behind!

Oak ran.

Ashe – protector, defender of his people – never once looked over his shoulder to see if they were following. He stopped to allow the clan to catch up only when he reached the ridge, and that was as shocking to Oak as the fight and the foul words that had streamed from the chief's mouth.

Feeling a strange and unfamiliar fear of his father, Oak stood some distance from Ashe as he watched the rest of the clan make its way up the slope. A baby – Oak couldn't see whose – was wailing at the top of its lungs, its mother in too much of a hurry to stop and soothe it. Rowan's litter had been abandoned and the sage was on foot, her hair disarrayed, her furs askew. The flowers in Lark's hair had wilted; one dropped sadly to the ground as she neared him. And where was Willow? There – at the rear, the shelter folded and packed into a bundle on her back – helping one of the infirm elders up the slope.

Oak watched his father count the matriarchs. When all the families were assembled, he simply grunted, then turned his back once more and led his clan away from the stones.

They pressed on silently, and as night gave way to day, Oak noticed Willow's red-rimmed eyes. She'd been crying, that much was clear. Her lip still quivered and her nose ran. It was another strange sight in a world turned upside down.

Not long after sunrise, the Goddess finally released her tight grip on the clouds. It rained, a gushing torrent falling from the sky, soaking everyone, streaming over the earth, turning every dip into a muddy puddle. It was the drought's end – surely that would improve his father's mood? But no … if anything it seemed to darken it further. Ashe was muttering to himself. Oak edged as near as he dared and thought he caught the words, "They were not right. They were not. I do not believe it."

Oak wanted to talk to Willow about their father, but when he approached, she turned aside, her lips tight pressed together as if she was scared of what might come out of her mouth.

"Are you angry with me?" he said.

"Go away, Oak."

"Is this because of last night? I was only playing."

"I said, go away."

Oak was desperate. Nodding towards their father, he said, "If you don't talk to me, I'll tell him what I saw."

Willow stopped. Opened her mouth then closed it again. They both knew it was an empty threat. No one wanted to go near Ashe while he was in such a strange mood. Shaking her head, she gave Oak a pitying look before turning away from him.

Well, if she wouldn't talk to him, there were others. He doubted Lark and Yew knew any more than he did, but at least they'd be better company.

He fell into step beside them. As the three of them splashed through mud, slipping over the wet grass, Lark whispered, "What's all this about, Oak? What's going on?"

"I don't know," he said.

Lark looked surprised. "Did the chiefs argue at the feast?"

"I don't know," he said again.

Lark gave an incredulous laugh. "But you were there – what did they say to each other?"

"Nothing! Nothing important." Oak wouldn't admit that he'd not been listening.

Yew spoke up. "Riff said..."

"Riff?" Oak interrupted. "What would he know?"

Lark raised an eyebrow. "More than you, it seems!"

50

Yew laughed.

Oak was nettled. "It's a pity he's not here to explain things then, isn't it? You obviously like him more than me."

"It's not a contest!" Yew protested. He was looking at Oak with the same pitying expression as Willow had. So was Lark.

"Why does everything have to be about you?" she asked.

The words were out before Oak could stop them. "Because it is! I'm the chief's son! I'll be your leader one day."

Yew and Lark exchanged another glance.

"You can lead anywhere you like," said Lark. "But whether we'll follow is up to us."

The rain stopped as suddenly as it had started, and soon the elders were complaining that it had been the wrong sort of rain. It had fallen too hard, too fast, like stones from the sky. The earth couldn't drink so much at one time. It would run off the sun-baked ground, they said as they continued their long journey home, and turn streams into rivers, rivers into torrents that would tear up trees by the roots, cause floods and catastrophes. There was much head-shaking.

Oak sighed inwardly. They were so predictable!

When he was chief, there'd be no teeth-sucking, no rolling eyes, no grumbling. All that would be banned. In his clan, people would be happy. They'd have to be, or they'd get cast out.

Ashe seemed strangely cheered by the brevity of the rain. A smile had taken hold of his face that didn't shift for the length of that day.

"One tiny storm! Is that all? The drought has not broken," he said, shaking his head. "Idiots. Fools!"

No one replied because he didn't expect them to. Ashe was talking to himself.

The journey home from the clan meet was both dreary and dangerous. The rain did indeed cause floods, just as the elders had predicted, and the going was so treacherous in places that they had to stop and wait a day or more for the water to recede. And then for long stretches the terrain was deathly dull, and it was simply a matter of setting one foot in front of the other while never seeming to get any closer to the horizon. Without Lark and Yew to keep Oak company, the time between sunrise and sunset seemed to last twice as long as it should. When he heard the two of them chatting and laughing, he raged against them. Why couldn't they just say sorry?

His father's peculiar mood did not alter for the

whole duration of the journey. If the elders discussed it, they did so too quietly for Oak to hear.

Food was increasingly scarce, though Oak himself did not go hungry. His stomach had only to rumble and Willow – from long habit, he supposed, for she was barely speaking to him – would press her own portion into his hands.

In previous years, arriving back on their mountain plateau after the thrills of the clan meet had always lowered Oak's spirits – home had seemed so dull in comparison. But this year, when he crested the brow of the last peak and saw Deer territory spread out below him, his heart soared.

There in the distance beside a glittering stream stood their domed huts, made from whips of willow stuck deep into the ground and plaited together overhead. The whips had taken root and grown with each passing moon, the bark fusing together. The structures were now so strong and solid they resembled a cluster of giant snail shells at the foot of the sacred mountain.

It seemed that the rains that had made the journey so difficult had been kinder here. Water had poured down from the mountains that ringed the plateau and then pooled, held in by the rock. While they'd been walking home, it had sunk deep into the earth and now the place was green and bright with fresh-sprung grass.

"Cursed?" said Ashe when he saw it. He laughed, but there was more sadness than mirth in it. "Oh Goddess! They are proved wrong."

As the clan crossed the plateau, it was plain that there were new-made hoofprints and that the grass was dotted with fresh animal droppings. Not just those of deer, either; there were piles of dung that Oak didn't recognize. He'd have pointed them out to Lark and Yew if they'd still been friends. He'd have asked Willow – the best tracker in the clan – what animal made them but she was still sulking. He dared not question his father. Oak had to remain in ignorance. But it was clear to him and everyone else that the herds on which they depended had returned.

So it came as no surprise when – the moment they reached the village, before any of them had even set down their bundles – Rowan sniffed the air and told the clan to prepare.

They would hunt at dawn.

PREY

A hunt! The prospect cheered everyone. For the first time since the midsummer meet, Ashe's smile looked joyful. When he gave a triumphant yell, Oak echoed it along with the rest of the clan.

As Oak put his sleeping sack down in their hut and untied his waist pouch, his skin prickled with excitement at what tomorrow might bring. He'd been allowed to go along on one hunt last autumn, creeping, freezing, stalking with Willow and the other hunters as they neared the herd. Then, as instructed, he'd hung back and lain motionless in the grass, barely breathing, while they closed in on their prey. It had been exhilarating even to be a small part of it. And then, oh, the thrill of the kill, the feast that had followed! Deer meat, roasted with juniper and thyme. Oak's mouth watered at the memory.

With luck, Rowan would let him go along tomorrow, although he wouldn't be allowed to hunt properly until he was counted a man. That was still two summers away.

And yet... A thought suddenly struck Oak.

This year was so different, the whole world had been flipped on its head. He'd stood beside his father at the clan meet.

Might it be possible...?

Oak's mind raced. At sunset the sage would enter the sacred mountain caves. There Rowan would pray to the Goddess, and Mother Earth would reveal where and what they would hunt.

And who would make up the party.

Suppose she named him? A fearful excitement tightened his chest. Why not? Though Willow was better at tracking, he could out-stalk his sister – he'd proved that, hadn't he, that final night of the clan meet? And if he could throw a stone with such accuracy, why wouldn't his aim with a spear be as good? The scene unfurled in Oak's head. He would prove himself the best hunter of them all! Willow would be proud of him. Yew and Lark would admire him and beg to be friends again. He'd be lauded and honoured by the whole clan.

He felt an urge to talk to his sister. She must have

forgiven him by now, surely?

When he found Willow, she was sitting a little way from their hut, fletching an arrow.

Oak squatted on his haunches near by, but she seemed in no mood to talk. How long would she keep this up for?

He said suddenly, "I didn't tell anyone about ... you know."

Willow looked at her brother, her brow contracted in puzzlement. Then she said, "Oh! That. I'd forgotten."

The moment the words left her mouth, her skin darkened. Even from where he sat, Oak could feel the heat radiating from her. She was lying. She lowered her head, giving her full attention to the arrow.

Oak tried again. "I didn't say anything."

Willow let the silence stretch out. And then she said quietly, "But you would have, if you'd thought it would be to your advantage." There was no anger in her voice. It was a simple statement of fact.

Oak was about to protest, but she lifted her face and stared at him. There was no point saying any more on the matter.

Willow sighed and shook her head. "You're such a baby." She wasn't teasing or mocking. Her voice was sad, not angry, and that made it many times worse. Oak's temper stirred, but before he could speak, Willow added, "It wouldn't matter what you said about me. Our father has more important things to worry about. Have you considered why he fought with Roc? Have you wondered why the Bear clan are now our enemies?"

Oak was thrown off balance. He sat down in the dirt. He'd thought about it, of course he had. But in truth he'd been more preoccupied with raging against Yew and blaming Lark for the rift that had grown between them.

"You see nothing but yourself," Willow sighed. "Not even when something is right under your nose! Look around you, Oak."

He was being tested. Slowly, Oak cast his eyes around the camp. His father was sitting alone, tying eagle feathers to the haft of his spear. Thorn was chipping away at the blade of his knife, sharpening it. Some elders were tending cooking fires; some were gossiping about great hunts of the past. Children were playing. Everything seemed normal. But he had the vague feeling that something was missing. What was it? A sense of failure descended on Oak as he looked blankly back at Willow.

Three words. That was all. Dropped like stones at his feet.

"Where is Fang?"

It was only when his tongue began to dry that Oak realized his mouth had dropped open and he was sitting there gawping like a seer in a trance. He snapped his jaw shut so suddenly, the tip of his tongue caught in his teeth. "Ow!"

Willow gave a bitter laugh.

Oak stood up. He didn't like this sense of … what? Wrongness.

Because where *was* Fang?

Oak searched Willow's face for an answer. "Tell me," he pleaded.

Willow looked at him for one, two heartbeats before dropping her eyes. "I don't know," was all she said. She turned back to her arrows and it was clear the conversation was at an end.

Why was everything so odd? Oak hated it. Nervous restlessness fizzed through his veins as the sun sank behind the mountains.

And then he saw Rowan walking towards the sacred caves, a crown of feathers in her hair, her ceremonial cloak so heavily hung with totems and beads of bone it clicked with each step. The tallow lamp in her hand illuminated a face daubed with sacred signs and symbols. Tonight the Goddess would speak to her alone.

Oak felt the sudden urge to follow.

TRESPASS

It was forbidden. The moment Oak set foot in the tunnel, he was treading on sacred ground, uninvited. The holy ritual was absolutely secret. Not even his father had seen it.

Outcast.

Trespass.

Punishable by death.

The words his father had hurled like weapons at the clan meet echoed in his mind.

But they didn't apply to him.

Whatever Oak did, the Deers could never make their chief-in-waiting an exile. As for the Goddess? She'd done nothing all those years ago when he and Willow had gone wriggling on their bellies through the grass to watch the midsummer ritual. If she hadn't struck him down then, why would she do so now? The thought was reassuring, but his pulse still raced.

The tunnel twisted. Turned. Soon there was no light from the setting sun behind him, and only Rowan's lamp ahead. As Oak crept forward, he felt the great weight of rock above him. Little by little he sensed the might of the Goddess, oppressive here in a way it wasn't in the open air. Every bone, every muscle, every nerve in his body began to whisper, *Turn back! Get out of here. Go!*

No. He wouldn't.

Couldn't.

Stupid Oak! He had no lamp and hadn't marked the way. He must stay close to Rowan or he'd be lost in the bowels of the mountain. He went on, his mind forcing his body onwards along one narrow tunnel and then another. Creeping. Freezing. Listening. Alert for any sign that Rowan sensed his presence.

Moving quietly came as no challenge to Oak, but he had no control over the noises his stomach made. Fear had set his insides gurgling and every sound was magnified.

He hung well back. In the blackness Rowan's light was easy enough to follow. When it stopped moving, Oak guessed that she had reached the sacred spot. He was still a stone's throw behind. Rounding that bend there – where the rock jutted out – he'd see the cavern and witness a ritual that was meant to be shared only between the Goddess and her human mouthpiece.

Heart thumping, Oak edged forwards. He did not hear the striking of fire-stones or the careful blowing of a spark into a flame, but suddenly there was the crackle of a fire taking hold and the smell of burning wood. It had taken no time at all! Dry kindling and timber must have been piled ready and waiting. It had caught at once, lit from the lamp, perhaps? Or maybe it was the breath of the Goddess that had set the fire roaring.

The sage was praying now, whispering to Mother Earth. He couldn't hear the words but assumed Rowan was asking for guidance, for a vision. As the flames rose higher, her chanting grew louder and more frenzied.

And then Oak felt a shift in the air. Solid rock seemed to shimmer and he had the strangest feeling that if he pressed too hard against it, he would slip through as easily as if it was water. The skin between the spirit and living worlds was stretching, splitting. He could not hear them, but he sensed the shades of his ancestors watching, waiting, whispering. He moved more quickly now towards the bend in the tunnel. Curiosity was stronger than fear. He had to see what Rowan did next.

He had reached the jutting rock. Taking a deep breath, balling his hands into fists, he peered around it.

Rowan was staring straight at him. The feather crown gave her the look of an eagle. Her gaze skewered him to the spot, punching air from his chest. Suddenly, the prospect of punishment was real and immediate. Goddess! What had he done?

But the sage didn't curse or even acknowledge him.

Through his panic he saw Rowan's lips moving and heard the chanting continue, uninterrupted, undisturbed. It was then he realized that her eyes – though they were on him – were glazed. She was not seeing the living world, but that of the spirits. Rowan was in a trance. The Goddess filled her head, steered her body.

Oak's terror abated, his breathing steadied. He watched as Rowan suddenly picked a branch from the fire, stamping out the flames that were consuming it. He smelled the searing flesh of her bare feet and had to clamp his hands over his mouth to stop himself gagging. Tears sprung to his eyes with the effort of not crying out. Yet Rowan showed no pain. Indeed, she seemed to feel nothing at all.

When the branch was a smoking, blackened stick, Rowan raised it and brought it down in a sweeping movement over the cave wall.

What was she doing?

Oak's eyes roamed the cavern. The rock was pale here – the colour of teeth or bone – the firelight warming it to a red glow. The walls were dancing with images of animals. The flickering flames gave life to them, making them seem to jump, to move, to run. There was an aurochs, a man impaled on its huge horns. Beech, father of Lark, had died just that way. How strange!

And over there – stranger still – was a herd of deer fleeing across the wall towards the entrance to the cavern where Oak stood. The flames flared and he saw that drawn behind them were hunters, a whole group of them, pursuing their prey. His heart leaped with recognition. They were simple sketches, a few charcoal strokes, that was all. And yet they were unmistakably people of his clan – those black lines had captured the spirit of each individual. There was Thorn, with the injured leg that made him twist sideways when he ran. Apple, with hunched shoulders and stumpy feet. Ashe, with hair that curled into ropes flying out behind him, the half-grown pup, Fang, running at his heels.

Fang. When had he last seen the dog?

He'd think about it later.

His eye was caught by the figure beyond Fang –

a girl, hair tied back, spear in hand, raised ready to plunge it into the deer.

Willow! Oak realized with wonder that he'd watched this very hunt! He'd seen exactly this scene play out last year. Ashe and Fang had driven the deer towards Willow and she'd killed one entirely on her own. She'd been praised to the stars for it.

Is this what Rowan did in the cave? Paint the images of past hunts? Why would the Goddess make her do that?

As he watched the sage, a new thought curled like a wisp of smoke into Oak's head. Was it possible that Rowan drew images not of the past, but of what was to come? Had she drawn Willow slaying the deer before that hunt took place? Was this the Goddess's foretelling, her promise of what would happen at daybreak? Oak trembled with awe at the idea.

If it was so... What was she doing now?

Rowan was scratching the burned stick across the wall. A new scene, new creatures, sprang into being.

Oak squinted. He could make no sense of the lines. It was prey, but it was something he'd never seen before. Larger than a deer, and heavier. But not bison. Not aurochs. It was running. Running fast. And then there was another appearing on the rock beside the first. Another, and another, fleeing from danger, their young running at their heels on stick-thin legs. And then one more, separate from the others, a black stripe running the length of its back, standing on its hind legs, the front ones thrashing the air. It was fighting for its life, that much was plain. But fighting what? Who?

Rowan took another branch and extinguished the flame. She drew the hunters now, bows in hands, the air thick with arrows. Others, with spears raised, were running after their prey. He could pick out Thorn. Ashe. Willow.

And another figure, there at the side, arms raised high. Oak's heart began to thud so hard against his ribs he was sure Rowan would hear it. She'd drawn him! It was him! He was there at the kill! Goddess! Would he be the one to slay the creature? Oak could almost hear its scream cut short, smell the blood gushing from the wound, feel it running down his arm.

Rowan stopped. There was a long silence and all Oak could hear was the seer's breathing and the crackle of the fire. Then Rowan cried out as if in pain. She was seized by a fit of shaking and, whirling around, she pulled a third branch from the fire. Crushing the flames, she walked to the far corner of the cave and, with sweeping, frenzied movements, drew something on the rock there.

And then it was over. Staggering back, she sank,

exhausted, onto the cave floor.

For a long time the sage lay still. Was she sleeping? Was she ill? He couldn't find his way out without her! Oak took a step towards the old woman. Her chest was heaving – she was still alive, thank the Goddess! A low moan leaked from her mouth and Oak hid himself once more as she emerged from the trance like a swimmer from deep water. Wearily, Rowan rose to her feet and looked at what she'd drawn on the cave walls, running her fingers across the images of the hunters, naming their names in a low, wondering whisper.

"Who do we have? Willow, I see you will hunt. As will Thorn and Ashe. I expected nothing less. But oh, Oak will join you! Very well."

The sage turned full circle and uttered a final prayer to the Goddess, giving thanks for the vision. It was only then she noticed her last drawing.

"What's this? What?"

Rowan limped to the corner of the cave. Peering forward to examine it she suddenly started.

"Alder!" she cried.

Alder? thought Oak. *Who's that?* He'd heard the name before but it wasn't anyone of the Deer clan. Oak was almost sure she muttered it again, but he couldn't be completely certain. Then Rowan screamed.

67

The dreadful sound bounced from wall to wall and back again. It circled like a wild thing. Oak half expected the animals to flee from the walls and stampede along the tunnel to escape the noise.

Rowan was out of breath. She fell silent, then stood up and began to stagger towards the entrance of the cave, hurrying to get out, to get away from whatever hideous vision was drawn on the wall, straight towards the place where Oak crouched.

He panicked. When he'd followed the sage here, he'd given no thought to the return journey. Rowan was close now. In a heartbeat she'd trip over him. He couldn't slip out ahead of her: he'd been running into pitch blackness. If he took a wrong turn, he'd be lost inside the mountain for ever.

He curled into the rock, tucking his face into his knees so the lamplight wouldn't catch the gleaming whites of his eyes. He was good at this, he told himself. The best in the clan! The eye is always drawn to movement, he reminded himself – the flight of a bird, the dropping of a leaf – if he stayed still as stone, Rowan's eyes would slide over him.

But this was the sage who could see past and future, who could see the world of spirits. She was bound to notice a boulder that hadn't been there before, wasn't she?

No! Thank the Goddess! Rowan sped past him as if a pack of wolves was snapping at her heels, too distressed by that last drawing to see the real world. For a moment Oak was tempted to cross the cave and see what had filled her with such horror. The fire was still burning; there was enough light. But he must hurry after her. If he didn't follow now, he'd never find his way out.

When Rowan finally emerged from the mouth of the cave and stepped into the moonlight, Oak hung back. It was only two stone's throws from the village, and though night had fallen he didn't want to risk being seen emerging from the sacred mountain. He watched her walk slowly towards the huts, apparently perfectly calm and composed. Ashe strode forward to meet her, head lowered to better hear what she had to say. The chief then shouted a command for his clan to gather by the fire. Only then – when all was hustle and bustle – did Oak slip out of the cave, keeping low to the ground, circling the huts at a run so he could approach from the opposite direction.

By the time he joined the clan he was out of breath and Rowan's prayer of thanks to the Goddess was well underway.

It was odd. He'd seen how troubled the old woman

was. Yet now her words, her delivery, her tone were the same as always. Rowan was hiding something.

As the sage began to chant a prayer, Oak's mind strayed back to the cave. The images of tomorrow's hunters had been clear enough, but what was their prey? A dim memory prickled at the back of his mind. A clan meet, when he'd been small. The Fox elders had been telling stories around the fire. Hazel, his Fox aunt, had talked of animals with gleaming coats of grey and black and brown, animals that had a crested ridge of hair running the length of their necks and flowing tails that hung down to their heels.

"And oh, those heels!" Rook, his Fox uncle had said. "Hard, hard hooves that can smash the skull of a man with one kick!" He'd spoken of flaring nostrils that billowed with smoke. Creatures that were larger than deer but fleeter of foot, and whose flesh was sweeter and more tender than any they had ever tasted. Young Oak had been captivated by the tales but dozed off soon after. In the morning he'd not been sure if those animals were something he'd dreamed.

Yet now ... those things Rowan had painted on the cave walls?

What had Hazel called those animals? The name came back to him a moment before it fell from the sage's lips.

"Horses," Rowan declared. "The Goddess has sent us horses."

The reaction was instantaneous. A murmur of excitement rippled through the clan. Horses were creatures of myth to the Deer people. They knew of their existence, but not even the elders had seen one. All around him Oak could hear whispers as they agreed that yes, of course, the drought must have forced the animals to seek new pastures here on the plateau. The herd must have ventured onto their territory because the Goddess had provided so much freshly sprung grass!

"You will find them at dawn at the place of the twisted pine," declared the sage. She then began to name the hunters: "Thorn, Raven, Linden, Willow, Sparrow, Damson, Apple, Linnet, Wren, Jackdaw..."

Oak's smile was rising; he felt it curling the corners of his lips.

"You will be led by Ashe, as always."

The chief bowed his head respectfully. "And for that I give the Goddess much thanks."

Soon Rowan would declare that Oak, son of Ashe, chief-in-waiting, would hunt for the first time. He would make his first kill. Oh, this was just the start! He would be better than all of them. He'd become the mightiest of hunters. But he must look surprised when the revelation came. Oak kept his face down so Rowan couldn't read the knowledge in his eyes.

He stood, waiting.

Rowan did not speak. The elders shuffled restlessly, wanting to go and make preparations but unable to leave until the sage gave the final blessing.

The moment drew out, longer and longer, a thread of silence that finally snapped.

"Oak," she said. "You will hunt too. Goddess protect you."

Swiftly she raised her arms high and gave the final blessing: "May the Goddess guide all your hands and ease your weapons' flight."

Even as Oak's heart soared, even as he punched the air in triumph, even as he whooped his joy into the night sky, a small part of him recognized something strange in Rowan's tone. Had he given it any consideration, he might have realized that she had not made the announcement as though it was something to be celebrated. No ... she had sounded almost as if she was relaying news of a tragic accident.

HUNTING

Oak was going to hunt! He was the youngest of his clan ever to win the honour. Graciously he accepted the congratulations offered by Lark and Yew. If their tone was a little cold, if they sounded slightly insincere, Oak didn't notice. His mind was full to bursting with happy imaginings. He would be admired. Respected. Revered. He'd be the kind of chief that poets sung about at clan gatherings: tales of his deeds would pass from mouth to mouth down the generations.

His sister appeared at his side, looking at him with eyebrows raised.

"I'm going to kill a horse!" Oak said before he could stop himself.

"Really?" she said, smiling. Leaning towards him, she whispered, "What with?"

Oh. Oak was instantly deflated. He had the same flint knife that all members of the clan carried. A bow and arrows, too, but really they were little more than playthings Willow had made for him when he was small. He'd never bothered fashioning full-sized weapons of his own. Why spend a day chipping a flint into an arrowhead when his sister was so much better at it than him? But now... He would need something good and sharp if he was going to bring down a horse single-handed! Yet it would be impossible to make anything overnight: not by firelight, not when he had so little skill.

"Idiot!" Willow laughed, not unkindly, and she put a hand on his shoulder. "Come on, little brother," she said, steering him towards their shelter. "Let's see what we can find."

A spear. A quiver of arrows, a new-strung bow. Willow supplied him with everything. And then the two of them sat and listened while their father talked. Ashe told Oak how he must behave, how he must follow orders and do exactly as he was told. The clan had never hunted horses before: they were an unknown prey, much more dangerous than deer. They must all work together if the hunt was to succeed. Ashe sighed, and a pained expression flitted across his face.

"I wish she was still alive," he said.

She. Oak's mother.

Ashe didn't say her name – those of the dead were never spoken by the living: it called them from the spirit world where there was neither hunger nor pain. It angered them.

Oak and Willow exchanged a glance but said nothing. Oak had never known his mother and Ashe was still so saddened by her loss that he mentioned her rarely. The silence grew longer and more awkward.

At last Willow reached out and laid a hand on her father's arm. It broke his trance. He smiled. "How like her you both are! I thank the Goddess for that. Your mother hunted horse before we married. If she was here now, she would know how best to make a kill."

"May the Goddess grant us her wisdom, then," said Willow. "And her skill."

The moment of sorrow had passed. Ashe declared it was time to sleep.

Oak's mind buzzed with secret knowledge. Not only was he going to hunt but he might even make the kill! And then? The feast they'd have! The strangeness of the past moon could all be forgotten. He'd make Ashe proud, and his father's mysterious rage would be obliterated. Lark and Yew would apologize and he'd forgive them. Everything would be as it had always been. Oak didn't expect to sleep, but when he lay in the familiar shelter for the first time in two moons, comfortable in his sleeping sack, his eyes closed almost at once.

He did not dream.

At first light, when Ashe shook him awake, Oak noticed the change in the wind. Throughout the long walk home it had blown relentlessly from the high mountains, carrying a whisper of ice rivers in its breath.

But now it came from a place Oak had never seen and could not imagine. It carried heat and dust and – what was that? – something strange. A scent, faint but unmistakably animal. Slightly sweet, a tang of fresh grass and honey. Sweat and musk... Not deer, not aurochs, not bison.

Was that the smell of horses?

Something stirred like a worm in his belly. Excitement or fear? He couldn't tell. This wasn't a fantasy any more, this was real. And yet, as he readied himself for what lay ahead, he'd never felt more like a sleepwalker in a dream.

In the greyness before sunrise the hunters assembled by the stream's bank. There they scooped handfuls of red clay and began to cover themselves with the sacred symbols that would honour the Goddess and bring good fortune.

Oak had watched the ritual so often. And yet what a difference there was between seeing something done and attempting it himself. His fingers felt clumsy and awkward as he daubed the shape of a blazing sun and crescent moon on his cheeks. The clay was cold and wet, making him shiver as he smeared lines representing the running river, the restless wind, the generous earth down each arm and across his torso. Between knee and ankle he drew the flickering flames of fire.

When the hunters were ready to depart, Ashe gave his orders. They were to proceed in the direction of the twisted pine. But before they reached it, the party would divide. Half would go to his knife-hand side and half to his heart side. He would lead Thorn, Apple, Linnet and Raven. Linden was to take Sparrow, Damson, Wren, Jackdaw and Willow the opposite way. They would spread out, encircle the herd and wait for his signal. Oak was to be the last in line. He must position himself by the jagged rock that stood a few stone's throws from the pine.

The hunters nodded. There was to be no more talking until they had made a kill. And now it was time to leave.

Keeping the wind in their faces, staying low to the ground, the hunting party moved swiftly, silently across the plateau. Oak copied Willow, bending almost double, rolling on the outside of his feet to spread his weight. The clay on Oak's skin dried and began to itch uncomfortably but he resisted the urge to scratch.

A mist was rising, wreathing its way through the grass, coiling into balls under the trees. The sweet smell of grass and honey and dung grew stronger; it was thick in Oak's nostrils, yet he could see no prey.

The twisted pine was barely within sight when Ashe gave the sign for the party to divide. Oak did as he'd been told, waiting until last. Then slowly he crept across the grass towards the jagged rock, his eyes scanning from one side to the other and back again. The mist swirled and gathered into more solid form. It was as if the Goddess was balling her breath like clay in her hands, shaping it...

With a jolt Oak realized that what he'd taken for patches of fog under the trees were in fact animals; grey as the mist, the hair that ran the length of their necks jewelled with droplets of dew.

Though the sun was lightening the sky, the creatures were sleeping still, babies lying stretched on the ground while their mothers dozed on their feet, ears flicking back and forth, checking for danger even as they dreamed.

Rowan's drawing had been of a herd in panic, trying to flee; galloping, squealing. A mass of blood and meat. They were simply prey. Something to fill the clan's bellies, if the Goddess willed it.

But this was different. A herd of horses, bathed in the early morning light.

Oak had never seen anything so beautiful.

He reached the rock as one by one the horses began to stir, stretching out necks, shaking hair, yawning. Awake, they were no less captivating. Soft greetings rumbled from their throats as they arched their necks, bringing noses close together, breath billowing like smoke from their nostrils. As the sun rose higher, he heard the tearing of grass, teeth grinding as they broke their fast.

From his hiding place he watched, entranced, all thoughts of killing momentarily gone from his mind.

He'd seen herds of deer and none but the stag was distinguishable. It was the same with bison or aurochs – each animal was an exact copy of the other.

Yet with these creatures, there was something distinct and individual about each of them. There was one that reminded Oak of his father; the way the animal carried itself, the way it looked about as if it was responsible for each and every member of its herd. This was the chief.

There – close beside it – was a female, long-faced with a dipped back and round belly. Though old, it was strong and all-seeing, all-knowing, like Rowan. The chief watched from the corners of its eyes, bowing to the old female's wisdom. When she called – a rumbling that sounded almost like laughter – the chief answered the call at once, approaching with head lowered respectfully. Then they stood shoulder to shoulder, each facing the other's tail, nuzzling, nibbling, scratching necks with their teeth.

There were many more horses than the fingers on both Oak's hands cropping the grass, intent on filling their bellies. Their babies kept close beside them.

But on the fringes of the herd was one that stood alone – not part of the group but near enough to feel its protection. It was a little smaller than the chief but didn't have the leggy look of the babies – one of last year's births perhaps? The other horses were pale shades of grey or nut-brown but this youngster was the same deep charcoal as Rowan's marks on the cave wall.

There was something teasing in its manner as it neared the babies.

The old female raised its head and grunted –
a warning? Who to? To the chief? To the youngster?

The charcoal horse was playing now, trotting
around the outside of the herd, tossing its head, kicking
up its heels. Dancing, prancing, squealing an invita-
tion to chase, to play. It ran rings around the others,
twisting, turning, changing direction. It flowed over
the grass with the speed of the wind and the smoothness of water. Yet none of the babies would join in.

It was brimful of energy, bursting with mischief.

The old female watched with disapproval. Oak
felt a kind of kinship for the youngster as it neared
the middle of the herd. It approached the old female
politely, lowering its head. They seemed to be blowing
breath into each other's nostrils and Oak wondered if
that was a greeting amongst horsekind.

The old female grunted and went back to grazing. But the youngster suddenly swung to the side and
nipped her hindquarters.

It was so daring, so cheeky, that Oak had to clasp
his hands over his mouth to stop a laugh escaping.

But the youngster had gone too far. The old female
squealed with fury and was transformed from wise
old matriarch into a wild, raging explosion of teeth
and hooves running at the youngster once, twice.

The youngster dodged and dodged again, leaping

aside at the last possible moment, revelling in its youth and agility, teasing, tormenting. Yet the old female persisted, running at it over and over, gradually driving the offender to the edge of the herd and then beyond.

The young horse seemed to realize the danger it was in. Suddenly it tired of its game. It lowered its head and its lip drooped and quivered as if in apology.

But the old female was not quick to forgive. The young horse was not allowed to rejoin the herd. Though its apologies grew more abject, it was driven further and further away, closer and closer to where Oak was hidden behind the rock.

At that moment the sun crested the mountain. The young horse was caught in a beam of golden sunlight and Oak saw the stripe that ran the length of its back.

His stomach heaved. This was the horse Rowan had drawn on the cave wall. This youngster was the creature he was surely destined to kill!

His skin prickled into bumps. Everything was in place. Every hunter was poised and ready. The moment had almost come. Ashe would soon give the signal.

But Oak was not prepared; his bow was still slung across his back! There was a slight twitching in the grass to Oak's heart side. That would be Willow edging forward. She was so close! She had seen, as he now could, that one lone animal, separated from its herd, would be much easier to bring down. She'd already have an arrow fitted to her bowstring. There was no time for him to do the same. But he had the spear, didn't he? He must use that. His palm was sticky with sweat and clay. He twisted, trying to get a better grip, but fumbled, banging the haft against the boulder he was crouching behind.

Clack!

Loud as a blackbird's call of alarm.

The youngster's head shot up. It tensed.

Oak couldn't wait for Ashe's signal. He must kill it. Now!

He leaped to his feet, spear in one hand, knife in the other. The eyes of boy and horse locked.

What's that?
Short face, eyes front. Blood stink.
Predator!
RUN!

The twang of Willow's bowstring, the hiss of her arrow, a grunt of effort as Oak threw his spear.

The young horse reared.

83

Willow's arrow should have pierced its windpipe. Instead, it glanced off its shoulder, slicing a shallow groove through its flesh. Oak's spear missed by an arm's length and thudded uselessly into the grass.

A moment's pause, then Oak blinked and the world erupted into chaos.

The herd fled, galloping away so hard and fast that their thudding hooves set the mountains shaking. Hunters sprang from their hiding places, running towards the young horse, cutting off any escape route. Willow raised her spear and thrust it at the creature's neck. But it reared a second time, wheeling around, hooves flailing, catching her beneath the chin. Hoof cracked against bone. Oak heard the snap of her jaw, teeth clashing together. Saw her head, flicking back. And then his sister was falling. Falling. Blood misting the air as the horse twisted again. Its herd had gone. It couldn't follow. The hunters were behind it and Oak was ahead.

It ran straight at him.

Oak's feet had turned to stone. He couldn't move. Nostrils flaring, breath billowing, the beast came hurtling towards him, all bone and muscle and brute strength. He would be trampled.

Oak put up his hands. To kill the horse? To stop it? To protect himself? A gust of flaming breath hit his face and then the animal brushed past him, its hair flicking across his cheeks. He must not let it escape! Oak stabbed blindly with his knife and the blade caught in something. The fingers of his heart-side hand closed on the creature's neck hair. His arm was almost ripped from the socket as the horse whipped him off his feet. But Oak didn't let go. He couldn't.

Entangled together, they ran, Oak stumbling as he was dragged alongside in a dizzying, bewildering blur of hooves and grass and trees and panic. Oak could see nothing but horse, hear nothing but horse, feel nothing but horse. He tasted its breath, its sweat, its blood, its fear. It ran and ran and – just as Oak thought he might faint with the pain and horror of it – it came to a sudden halt.

Wheezing, shuddering, Oak tried to free himself but his hand was clenched into a claw. The horse's neck hair was wrapped around his fingers, biting into the skin. The creature's blood mingled with his own.

A roaring filled his head. He thought it was his blood rushing in his ears but then he realized it was the river. They had reached the place where the waters boiled and frothed before falling the height of many men into a deep pool.

If they had been left alone, he might have been able to separate himself from the terrified creature, but then the cries of hunters came from behind. He heard his father, yelling his name.

And it was Ashe's voice that did it. Though the river raged, the horse took a great leap forward, carrying Oak with it.

Water closed over their heads for one, two heartbeats before boy and horse broke the surface. Rolling, turning over and over in the torrent, hurled against rocks, they were swept downstream. And then they plunged over the waterfall – and for Oak the world went black.

PART II

HORSE

LOST

Was he dead?

No. There was too much pain. Head pounding, muscles aching, hand... What had happened to his hand?

Oak kept his eyes shut. He was dreaming, he told himself; feverish, lying in his hut having a dreadful nightmare. If he called Willow, she'd bring him something to ease his hurt. She'd spoon broth into his mouth, tell him all would be well.

He was soaking wet. It must be raining. The drought had broken at last and the roof was leaking so badly the whole floor was awash. Any moment now Ashe would mend it. That terrible noise of someone having trouble breathing, that wheezing, snorting sound that he could feel vibrating through his body, making his teeth rattle ... it was just his father snoring. Nothing was wrong.

Everything was wrong.

Flashes of the hunt came like lightning bolts behind Oak's eyes.

No matter how hard he tried, he could not wish himself home and safe.

The first thing Oak noticed when he opened his eyes was that the sun had leaped across the sky. It was already late afternoon! How long he had been out of his senses? Was it even the same day? He was in the river still, but it had broadened so much he could barely see the sides.

Everything familiar, everything he knew, had vanished.

Terror tightened his throat and loosened both bladder and bowels. His head pounded. He must have struck it on a rock. How badly was he hurt? He tried to raise his heart-side hand but it was still tangled in the horse's hair, cut, bruised and swollen.

He was lying belly down on the creature's back, face resting on its neck, nose almost brushing its ears. The animal was carrying him as it swam. He felt the thrashing of its legs, heard its laboured breathing, sensed its desperation to get to the shore. But they were in the grip of a fast-flowing current and it was all the horse could do to stay afloat.

Chilled to the marrow and dizzy with pain, Oak couldn't do anything but pray.

But not to the Goddess. The prayers that formed in his head were to his father. *Help me! Find me! Get me out of this! Take me home!*

Oak could feel the horse tiring beneath him, losing strength. It couldn't swim for ever. And if it sank? He'd be dragged down with it. He would enter the spirit world. Meet the mother who'd died giving life to him. But she was a stranger. He didn't want her; he wanted his sister!

Willow! Was she all right? He'd seen her fall, seen her blood, misting the air. *Goddess! Keep her safe.*

Now the river seemed to be playing with them. It spun the horse full circle, first one way and then another. It batted them both against rocks, then tugged them away.

And then something bumped against the horse's side – an ash tree, ripped from its roots from somewhere upstream. The weary animal lifted its head and placed its chin on the bark, resting while they drifted, held up by the trunk.

After travelling like this a long time they came to a bend in the river and a whirling eddy pushed them to a place where the current ran less strongly. The horse, feeling the water's grip weaken, used the last of its strength to swim towards the bank.

A sudden jolt as one hoof and then another struck the riverbed. Slowly, gradually, it staggered from the water exhausted, Oak astride its back. Its legs shook and it collapsed onto its knees. And now, only now, did Oak manage to find the knife he'd plunged harmlessly into the thick mass of the creature's neck hair and cut loose the fingers of his trapped hand. He slipped from the animal's back and it rolled onto its side. Oak sank down beside it, aching, bruised, shivering – yet alive.

For a moment he felt relief. But only for a moment.

He lay staring up at the sky in confusion. The river was in front of him. But the sun was setting in the wrong place. It should be on the other side of the water, not behind him. Had the Goddess turned the earth around?

Sudden realization squeezed the air from his lungs.

He was on the far bank of the river.

Lost.

Alone.

In enemy territory.

Because if the sun was setting *there*, and the river was *there*, this had to be Bear clan land. Before the clan meet there would have been nothing to fear. But now he was trespassing. For reasons Oak didn't know and couldn't understand, Deer and Bear were deadly enemies. The world was turned upside down. What punishment might the Bears inflict on him for straying into their territory?

He curled into a tight ball, wishing himself anywhere but here, wishing himself dead rather than alive and afraid. And alone.

Alone!

Oak had never, ever been entirely on his own. The enormity of the situation squeezed his stomach so hard that he vomited, retching and retching even when there was nothing left to bring up. Afterwards he lay trembling, his mind flooded with fear.

A boy without a clan was nothing. No one.

A boy without a clan was easy prey.

The sun was sinking fast but there were no elders tending cooking fires, no tallow lamps lighting huts, no flaming torches to keep wolves or lynxes at bay. He was sick and hungry, and there was no one to tend to him or give him food. No sleeping sack to keep him warm. No Willow, telling stories by the fire. No Ashe, watching over them both.

He gulped in air, tried to think. He should be practical and do what he needed to survive. Make a shelter. Light a fire. Clean the wounds on his head and hands. He'd been shown how often enough but he'd never really paid attention. There had always been someone else to do these things. Even when Ashe had insisted he start a task, there was always someone willing to finish it for him. He didn't know where to begin.

He felt helpless as a newborn. Why hadn't he drowned? Why hadn't the water taken him while he'd been unconscious? It would have been easier than this!

Oak sobbed. A chief's son should have more dignity, but he couldn't help it. There was no one to see. No one to care. Why hadn't they come to rescue him? Where were they?

Horse longed to rest. But the strange creature that had reared from the grass and stayed up on its hind legs, the thing that was neither lion nor lynx but undoubtedly predator, the stinking-of-blood creature that had seized his mane and clung to his back like a tick when they plunged into Galloping Water would not shut up! So much noise! It was howling like a wolf one moment, bellowing like a bison the next.

And he was so tired!

Be quiet, Thing! Be quiet.

The horse sighed heavily. It sounded disapproving and Oak was suddenly furious.

"This is your fault," he said. "Go away!"

He was being ridiculous and he knew it, but that only made him more angry. The animal was staring at him, looking down its long nose in contempt, and being despised by the creature that had caused the catastrophe was unbearable.

"Go away! Go away!" Oak got to his feet, waved his arms, tried to drive the wretched animal off.

Though the horse stood up, it retreated only a few steps before lying back down.

Oak was the hunter; the horse his prey. It should be afraid but he couldn't even scare it! He was useless.

He turned his back on the animal. The night sky had never looked so vast and he'd never felt so small. Though the air was warm, he shivered uncontrollably as he had when he'd emerged from the lake. He didn't even have a cloak to wrap himself in and there was no Willow to chafe his hands warm and keep him company. Suppose she was dead?

No! He mustn't think that: he'd lose his mind. Oak tried to keep calm, but every noise was magnified, every gust of wind felt like a predator's breath on his skin. As the last of the light faded, the boy sank to the ground and fell into an exhausted sleep.

WAKING

It was a warm night. The air that dried the horse's coat also drew the river water from Oak's tunic and warmed his chilled limbs.

At sunrise he was woken by birdsong. Not tuneful blackbirds, or larks rising skywards, pouring their sweet song down upon the earth. These cried sorrowfully to each other as if grieving some mysterious loss. What were they? He'd never heard calls like that before.

Aching from the roots of his hair to the tips of his toenails, Oak was aware of a sticky, bloody wound throbbing at his temple. Flies buzzed around his head, and the hand he put up to swat them away felt too large, his fingers so stiff he could barely move them.

Oak tried to fall back into unconsciousness but sleep would not take him.

His skin itched all over and his back was sore. He'd fallen asleep with bow and arrows still strapped across it and the quiver's knots had pressed into his flesh. And as many insects as there were stars in the sky seemed to have feasted on him in the night. Thirst made his throat ache. That was easily solved, he thought with a bitter laugh: there was plenty of water close by. But he was also hungry and there was no one to provide him with food.

Oak lay for a long time staring up at the clouds, trying to ignore his discomfort, praying for the Goddess to pick him up in her hand and carry him home. But she didn't. And as his stomach began more noisily to demand attention, slowly, reluctantly, Oak sat up. His movement startled the horse, and instantly it was on its feet: alert, afraid, wary.

Oak couldn't bear to look at it. He averted his eyes.

What was he to do?

The shadow of a memory fell across his mind. Willow, trying to teach him how to shape flint into an arrowhead. Him – in a temper because it took too long, it was too difficult – throwing his work in the dirt. His sister picking up where he had left off, saying gently, "One chip at a time. One here. Then another." She'd grinned at him and said, "It's like everything, brother. Solve the first problem before you worry about the next."

"You're right," he said now, aloud. What was his first problem? Thirst.

So drink.

It was strange. He'd thought he and the horse had been washed up on the bank, but now it seemed they were on a small island in a vast area of marsh. Last night, before sleep had claimed him, the water's edge had been close. Yet now it was several muddy paces away. And last night the river had seemed so wide that he couldn't see the far side. Now it was not one, single body, but many, many streams, running between great banks of shingle and mud and reed. Surely a river could not change so drastically! He must have been too tired to see things properly, that was all.

The river water tasted strange. It was not cold and clear like the streams of home but grey, silty. And there was a strange tang to it that made his tongue tingle. He took only a mouthful or two – enough to quench his thirst until he could find a fresh stream.

Oak turned his attention to food. He must eat. Food would give him strength, and with strength he could think more clearly. He could make a plan.

Every member of the clan – from the smallest toddler to the most aged elder – carried a pouch at their waist stuffed with the essentials anyone would need to survive. Fire-stones, a water vessel, a little food. Oak had always carried his more for show than anything: he'd never needed to use it before now. With clumsy fingers, he started to untie the knots. The river water had stiffened the hide and it was hard to work them loose. When he opened the pouch, he saw the fire-stones safe enough, but the dried meat and berries Willow had put in long ago were swollen and squashed into a pulpy mass. Any flavour they'd possessed had probably been washed away the day before, but he was too hungry to care. He took a handful and forced himself to chew slowly. He must not eat it all at once, he told himself. This might have to last him until he got home.

Home! Which direction was that? He was utterly lost. Goddess, how was he to find his way? Fear began to squeeze his stomach.

No! Don't think too far ahead. One thing at a time. Food. When the pouch is empty, how will you feed yourself?

He was good at stalking. If he spotted any prey, he would be able to creep up on it. But what then? He could throw a stone accurately enough, but with a sinking feeling he admitted to himself that with a bow he was a poor shot. Despite his father's nagging he'd never taken the time to practise his aim. He could creep and freeze well enough, but the chances of him hitting anything with an arrow were slim.

There was the horse, of course. It was there, close enough for him to try. But it would fight and he'd seen what those hooves could do. Willow. Blood misting the air. Had she...? No, he could not think it! And surely he'd know, deep down, if his sister had left this life? The sun could not rise on a world without Willow in it. He needed to get back to her to see she was all right.

He stared at the horse, wondering if he could slay the creature. But it was so big! There was enough meat on it to feed the whole clan, and he was alone. Oak knew well enough that if an animal gave its life, nothing must be wasted. Even if by some miracle he managed to kill it, the monumental task of butchering the thing, of stripping the guts and removing the organs, of skinning it, of curing the hide, of slicing the meat and drying in the sun whatever he didn't eat immediately – it would take days even if he was skilled at the task. And he was not. He sighed, realizing again how often he'd wriggled out of tasks, how much he'd left for others to do. He wouldn't even know where to start. No ... he could not kill the horse. It would be another offence against the Goddess and he'd already offended her enough.

He would have to find other food, but the landscape

around him was strange, the plants unfamiliar. There would be berries on bushes at home, but they would be green at this time of year and he knew all too well that unripe fruits could bend a person in two with stomach ache. There'd been that clan meet a few summers ago when a boy from the Raven people had given him a handful.

"Dare you!" he'd said.

Oak had taken the berries, but before he could raise a single one to his mouth, Willow had stepped in.

"Don't," she said. "They'll give you bellyache."

And what had the Raven boy said? Oak couldn't remember but it had driven Willow into a fury. She'd taken the dare on her brother's behalf, swallowing the things whole without even biting as they were so bitter. Then she'd spent the night curled on her side, arms clutched over her belly, not making any complaint, not making any sound at all but unable to hide the sweat that broke out on her forehead.

Was she lying like that in the hut now, hurt and injured?

Tears began to prick his eyes.

Don't think about that, he told himself. *Not now. Not yet. You have drunk. You have eaten. What's next? Home. How are you going to get home?*

He looked about him. A mist was rising and he

couldn't see anything distinctly. There was the river. The land beyond seemed solid and flat. And those shapes in the mist – was that a copse of trees?

Trees. Something jarred in his head. At clan meets, there on the open plain ... hadn't Ashe often joked about how fearful the Bear clan were to be under the wide sky? How they seemed to feel naked without a canopy of leaves? Didn't they favour the forest?

The land just here was open to the sky, like the sacred plain. Though this was undoubtedly their territory, perhaps – was it possible? – they didn't come to this part of it? The thought cheered him a little.

He recognized nothing of the landscape: there was no curve of hill, no twisted tree, no rock, nothing that was familiar. And with that river mist there were no distant landmarks on which he could fix his eyes as a guide. Willow always knew which direction was north, even on a cloudy night with her eyes shut, but he didn't have that same skill. There was only the river to guide him, and rivers twisted and turned like eels, they plunged through gorges and disappeared into caves and could not be trusted to go by the most direct or passable route. It had carried him so far! But if he walked against its flow, surely it would eventually guide him back home?

Oak turned towards the copse in the distance that he hoped indicated dry, solid ground, but the horse was blocking his path. He took a step towards it, assuming it would run off, but it simply backed away. Oak stepped to his heart side but the horse did the same. He dodged to the knife-hand side but the horse mirrored his actions. Once, twice more they danced this way and that, like two people trying to pass each other on a narrow track. The comic absurdity of it made Oak laugh suddenly. He raised his hands as if in apology.

And, bafflingly, the horse swung round and began to walk ahead of him towards the trees.

Without the protection of his herd, Horse was afraid. He had to get back. Though he couldn't see or hear or smell them, he knew they were that way.

Go!

Can't.

Can't get past Thing!

It was rearing again. And its strange front legs – legs that twisted and turned in the wrong directions – were waving in the air. Those hooves! Changing shape, bunched tight one moment, then opening like spiders. Like claws! Claws that might scratch. Might kill.

Thing was barking like a wolf, walking like a bird, flexing claws, coming towards him. Horse backed away, but on it came, stalking, driving, chasing him into mud that sucked at his hooves and tried to drag him down.

Oak gave the horse little thought, following his own path until he slipped, one leg sinking thigh-deep into the soft, sucking mud. He realized then that the animal – though no doubt heavier than him – had not sunk any lower than its knees. It was sniffing the ground, picking out a safe route to the shore.

After that, he followed in its footsteps.

As boy and horse waded on, the sun rose higher, but the mist – rather than burning off – became thicker. Oak lost sight of the copse. All he could see was mud and reeds and water and the horse's tracks. In the strange, dreamlike landscape, Oak began to wonder if the animal was a guide sent by the Goddess. How was he to feel about the creature?

It had certainly saved him from drowning. But it had wounded his sister, perhaps mortally.

He pushed the thought from his mind again. One thing at a time. One step at a time. Although each was becoming more difficult than the last, as little by little, there was less mud and more water.

Oak was wading through it almost waist-deep by the time he saw dry land.

Dry land, but not much of it. The horse had led him to another island. Grassy, with a single tree, but cut off from the mainland by another stretch of deep water.

Oak was tired. The day was uncomfortably warm and humid and the walk had been hard going. His legs ached. He decided to sit for a while, his back to the tree. The horse watched him, but after some time it lowered its head and began to crop the grass.

Horse was confused. Thing had driven him away from his herd, stalked him, like a predator. But now it had stopped on solid land where there was fresh grass. Thing was looking across the water, alert for danger. It was like a stallion, guarding his herd while they grazed. And he was so hungry!

Eat?

Eat!

Oak's head ached and his hand throbbed. His fingers had been lacerated when they'd been tangled in the animal's neck hair, and the wounds were hot – there was a risk of them going bad. The thought of becoming feverish, of being taken sick out here all alone, made him quail. He threw back his head and uttered a prayer to the Goddess to help. And then realized she already had. The horse had guided him to this place. He was sitting beneath a willow tree! And didn't Rowan boil the bark of willow into a brew that eased pain and fever? Sometimes when the clan was on the move and Oak was complaining of sore feet, she'd cut a strip of bark and give him that to chew.

Oak took his knife. Thanking the tree, apologizing for wounding it, he cut a twig and chewed the end. After some time the throbbing eased and became more bearable.

His eyes fell on the horse and its ear flicked in his direction, aware he was watching but continuing to graze. But something was bothering it, he realized. It swished its tail, sending a cloud of flies into the air that soon returned. It shuddered and stamped, the whole of its hide twitching with irritation. Oak sympathized. The wound on his own forehead was attracting their attention too. As the horse swung its head, he saw the groove across its neck where Willow's arrow had carved a path through flesh.

It had stopped bleeding, but Oak knew with a sickening certainty that if nothing was done very soon, flies would lay their eggs in the wound and maggots would burrow deep into living flesh. He'd seen animals eaten alive that way, from the inside out, and the sight had turned his stomach.

Was there anything he could do?

How had Rowan treated wounds? Clay, that was it! She'd balled up red clay and smeared it across the cut. It had cooled the skin, soothing and protecting the wound so the flies couldn't get to it.

The mud he'd waded through was not red, but it was sticky. Would it work the same way? He stared down at it and noticed that where the roots of the tree met the water's edge there was a seam of the red clay that he knew from home. He took a handful and smeared it across his forehead. Could he get close enough to the horse to do the same? If he didn't, the animal would suffer.

Scooping up another handful of clay, Oak walked towards the horse.

Horse was even more confused. Thing had behaved like herd, watching, protecting him from danger while he grazed. But now Thing was coming at him, one hoof bunched into a claw.

Run!

Can't!

Deep water surrounded the island, and the

thought of being in that sucking, drowning torrent again was unbearable.

Was Thing predator? Stalking? Hunting? Trying to kill?

No... No teeth, no claws... Thing did not pounce or bite.

It seemed like herd. What was it doing, then? Driving him out? Banishing him, like Old Mare had done? Why? He'd done nothing bad. But Thing seemed angry.

Round and round they went, first in one direction, then the other.

"I'm trying to help you," Oak muttered through gritted teeth. "Can't you see that? Why are you being so stupid?"

Oak got hotter and crosser chasing the animal this way and that, trying and failing to draw closer. Before long he was out of breath and out of patience. By then the creature was lowering its head and chewing its lip. He'd seen it doing exactly that when the old female had been driving it away from the herd, just before everything had gone so catastrophically wrong. What did it mean?

He didn't know. And just then he was too exhausted to care. Oak couldn't chase it any more. He didn't even want to look at it. He sat down under the tree to rest.

It was there that he noticed something strange. The groove he'd gouged through the red clay was now under the water. The river level had risen, the edge had moved closer. How was it possible? There hadn't been a rainstorm, and this wasn't floodwater.

He was staring at it, perplexed, when he felt hot breath on his neck. And then the horse was pressing its forehead against his spine.

BONDING

Thing is herd. Need herd.
Need Thing.
Sorry. Sorry!

For several heartbeats horse and boy stood, unmoving. Oak could feel the animal's breath on his calves, short and shallow puffs, as if nervous. Yet here it was, standing right behind him.

The clay was still in Oak's hand but it was warm now, caked between his fingers, too dry to press into the animal's wound even if it would let him.

What should he do next? He seemed balanced on the brink of something extraordinary. He must not throw it away.

Instinct warned him not to touch the animal. Not

yet. He didn't even look over his shoulder. Instead, he went to the water's edge and slowly, slowly, slowly squatted down to moisten the ball of clay in his hand. The horse took a step closer.

Oak found himself humming the soft, melodic tune Deer mothers sung to soothe their babies to sleep. No doubt his own mother had once sung the same to Willow. Never to him, though. She'd died too soon for that.

He felt the horse's ears flick forwards, the tips brushing his back. It was listening.

Oak kept up the humming. He thought of his father. Ashe had spent whole days watching the pack of dogs that hung about the fringes of the camp, trying to learn and understand the way they communicated with each other. He'd made a friend of Fang by throwing scraps whenever he ate, and soon the pup had followed him like a shadow.

Ashe had shared his observations about the dogs with Oak and he had listened, though with little interest. If he was honest, he resented his father's obsession.

Stupid! he thought now. *Jealous of a dog?*

"Staring any animal straight in the eyes is a challenge," Ashe had said. "A threat. It will drive it away. If you want to make friends, keep your face turned aside, look from the corners of your eyes."

Now Oak stood, moving so carefully his knees shook with the effort. And then, gently, one hair's breadth at a time, as if he was playing the stalking game, he turned and regarded the horse sideways. It stood its ground, but he could see tension in every muscle. One wrong move and it would leap out of reach, its fragile trust shattered. If the first time he touched it was to slap a handful of wet clay into an open wound, it would run. He had to be careful.

Still humming, Oak turned until he was shoulder to shoulder with it, facing the animal's tail. The wound was on the far side. That was good. He'd get to it later. Meanwhile he had to make the creature relax. He leaned in until the skin of his upper arm brushed its hide.

Its muscles contracted, ready for flight. But it didn't move away.

He'd seen the herd relaxed before the hunters burst from the grass: the horse chief and the old female rubbing each other's necks with their teeth. Could he do something similar with his fingers? Keeping his arm pressed against the animal, slowly, slowly he raised his heart-side hand, brushing the back of it across the horse's ribs until his fingers were where neck met spine. And then he shifted his balance so he could reach under that thick hair. He began to scratch.

The creature was surprised to begin with. Uncertain. Oak kept scratching, digging in his fingernails. And then – to Oak's delight – its lower lip began to sag, its eyes half closed in appreciation. Its top lip twitched and flicked and a little while later it was doing the same to him, scratching between Oak's shoulder blades with its teeth.

What had seemed so impossible before became an easy task. Humming softly, Oak took a step back and then, keeping his eyes down and his movements slow and smooth, twisted under the horse's head to get to its other side. He continued to scratch until the horse was once more doing the same to him. He kept it up while he raised his knife-side hand. And, with one firm, smooth swipe, he smeared the clay across the wound.

The horse felt it but merely gave a snort and a blink, because the boy had done it so swiftly and had carried on with the humming and scratching the whole time.

Now a smile spread across Oak's face. He felt quite ridiculously pleased with himself. For the first time he understood his father's fascination with the pup. To watch another creature, to begin to understand how it thinks, why it behaves the way it does – yes, there was a magic to it. He wished Ashe could see him.

A wave of homesickness suddenly crashed over Oak. Tears spilled from his eyes and, resting his head against the animal's neck, he let them flow.

LEADING

Standing with his forehead pressed to the horse's neck, Oak began to sense the animal's longing for its own herd. Knowing it was as lonely and afraid as him was peculiarly comforting. Somehow it gave him strength and courage. Oak wiped his face dry with the back of his hand and took a deep breath. And it was then that he saw there was something terribly wrong with the river.

While he'd been busy with the horse, the mist had burned away. Oak had one hand resting on the horse's shoulder and he was glad of its support because shock weakened his knees. The entire river – which now covered all the mud he'd waded through that morning – had stopped moving. It lay still as the mountain lake, the vast blue sky reflected so clearly that it was hard for a moment to tell which way was up.

Oak drew in another deep breath and then slowly exhaled and the water remained motionless. It was as if the Goddess had frozen it. And yet... No. He'd heard that even ice rivers high in the mountains of the far north moved onwards one finger's breadth at a time, creaking and cracking and sometimes falling, great cliffs of ice tumbling to the ground. But this? This stillness was uncanny. He stared, transfixed. And as he watched, almost imperceptibly the river started to move again.

But in the other direction.

He almost forgot to breathe. His mouth was dry.

He watched, dumbfounded, reluctant to believe his own eyes. Were they playing tricks on him? No... The river really was flowing the opposite way. How could that be? What was the Goddess doing to it?

As he stared, he saw that little by little the level of water in the river was dropping, as if a gigantic drinking vessel were gradually being drained.

Willow had told him a story when he'd been small enough to sit on her lap. She'd whispered a magical tale into his ear of when Mother Earth was young. Everything had been fresh, new-born, perfect, until a monstrous creature emerged from deep in her belly with a raging thirst. It drank all the streams, the rivers, the lakes. The plants withered and the animals died for lack of water and the earth herself would have perished had it not been for Zelak, the wondrous child who went in search of the creature. Armed with no more than a single feather, Zelak leaped into the monster's mouth and tickled its throat until all the water was spewed out on the earth again.

It was a story meant to while away a long winter's evening, that was all. And yet here he was, looking at a river that was slowly disappearing. Oak's mind began to race. Was that the reason for the drought? Had something drunk all the water from the sky? Had it now started on the river?

The thought of a monstrous creature squatting somewhere near by made his head spin. And then another thought occurred to him. Was this the Goddess's doing? Had she brought him and the horse to this place for a reason? Was he a second Zelak, meant to save Mother Earth from death?

No! That was ridiculous. Hunger was addling his brain. No one person could save the whole earth just as no one person could destroy it! It wasn't possible.

As he sat, trying to puzzle out what was happening to the river, the wind changed. A strange smell was carried on it, a tang that was unfamiliar but not unpleasant. It carried a strange noise, too, a far-distant rushing, sucking roar. Rhythmic. Persistent. As if, indeed, a monstrous creature was gulping down the contents of the river.

What was it? Should he go and see? He'd rather go straight home. But without the river's current as his trustworthy guide, he didn't know which way to turn. Goddess! Why hadn't he paid more attention when Willow and his father had tried to teach him the ways of Mother Earth? Had he been walking in the wrong direction all morning? He was utterly lost and had no idea at all what to do next.

Thing had stopped moving. Why? Horse wanted more grass. He wanted fresh water and Thing should have been sniffing it out and showing the way. But it wasn't.

Is it Leader? Or am I?

Ask.

Horse trotted around Thing, head high.

Follow me, Thing? Follow me?

No answer.

Ask again.

Horse stamped. Tossed his mane. Trotted in another circle.

Thing still didn't move.

Thing is herd.
But who is Leader?

Oak didn't know whether to laugh or cry. The horse was prancing around him, snorting, stamping, dancing almost. It was a very fine display, but what in the name of the Goddess was it doing? Threatening? Challenging him? It circled one way and then the other and then it stood, head raised, staring down its nose at him.

The creature reminded Oak of that boy from the Raven clan when he'd held out the handful of berries. What had he said that made Willow swallow them? He'd called her a coward, that was it. And she'd been prepared to suffer a night's bellyache to prove she wasn't.

He sighed. Willow was so brave, so clever. She hadn't needed to prove anything – not to the Raven boy, not to anyone. She'd eaten those berries to protect her baby brother. How many times had she done that throughout his life?

Oak's decision was made. He knew exactly what Willow would do if she found herself in this situation and he would do the same. She'd walk towards that strange crashing roar and so would he. If there really was a creature at the end of it, well, so be it. He would do what he must. And if he survived, if he ever got home ... he would have a story to tell his sister, one to make her proud.

His heart beat faster. Stronger.

He turned away from the horse and waded through the ebbing water towards solid land.

For some strange, inexplicable reason, the horse followed him.

Thing is Leader!
Happy!
Safe.
Thing lead.
Horse follow.

EXPLORING

The land was flat, the sky vast. Oak felt sure the Bears did not venture here, but he watched as he walked, alert for signs of human activity. What would he do if he found the remains of a cooking fire? Or – Goddess forbid! – if he came face to face with one of them? *Don't think about it,* he told himself.

Far ahead was a line of low hillocks no higher than burial mounds. Whatever was making the roaring noise lay beyond them. Oak walked. The horse snatched mouthfuls of grass as it followed, and when they came across a near-dried pond, both drank deeply. Pulling the boar's bladder vessel from his pouch, Oak filled it for later. The sun sank lower in the sky and the river gradually emptied until it was little more than a series of rivulets trickling between banks of mud.

As Oak drew nearer to the hillocks, the strange smell grew stronger, catching in his throat. The ground underfoot changed from dark earth to something of a much lighter hue. Oak scooped a handful and let it run through his fingers. It was stony but very fine, as though pebbles had been ground into flour. The land was less fertile here, the grass thinner and coarser, and Oak saw that the mounds which had looked so solid from a distance consisted of shingle held together by clumps of reed. He climbed the first, the ground slipping and shifting underfoot, his feet sinking deep. Sliding back a little with each step, he had to work twice as hard to get half as far. He crested the first hillock and slithered down the other side. Another rose before him and then another. With each one he climbed, the roaring noise grew louder.

When he reached the summit of the last, he gasped aloud.

The child's part of his mind had imagined a monstrous creature drinking the river, one with scales and wings, one that breathed fire and could fly like a bird. What lay before him was something entirely different, but no less alive and no less astonishing.

A great, flat expanse of shingle. And beyond it? A body of heaving water, crashing and roaring as it writhed and rolled itself against the land. It stretched all the way to the horizon, where it melted into the sky. Goddess! He could see the very edges of Mother Earth!

Overawed, heart pounding, Oak skidded down the final slope and walked towards it. As he drew closer, the ground underfoot grew wetter, and soon he was leaving sucking tracks that filled with water each time he pulled his foot free.

When Oak reached the rolling waves, he paused a moment before wading in, cupping his hands together and scooping some to his mouth. *Eurgh!* He spat it straight back out. This water – though there was so much of it – was not good to drink.

As he stared at it, mystified, he realized someone – no, something – was staring back at him. A head had emerged from the water and a pair of liquid brown eyes were taking a long, steady look at him. It seemed to lack ears but there was something dog-like about it that reminded Oak of Fang.

It lost interest in the boy soon enough but clearly found his companion fascinating. The horse snorted and the water-dwelling animal snorted back. The horse tossed its head and the water creature pointed its nose skywards and slipped under the water. It reappeared moments later, closer to the shore, scratching its head with a strange, flat paw. The horse snorted again and gave a low, rumbling call which the water animal replied to with a bark. The two seemed to converse awhile but then it dived beneath the surface once more.

Oak watched for a long time but it had gone. He stared across the rolling water and realized that – as there had been with the river – there was a moment of change. A pause, as if it was gathering itself, and then it started to advance back across the flat shingle, wave by wave. He watched until he was certain. Yes ... now it was edging towards the low hills. And a stone's throw away over there it was pouring into the river's mouth. If it carried on, in time it would overpower the river itself, changing the direction of its flow.

Of course! That's why the level had risen and fallen! The rolling water had indeed first swallowed the river and then spewed it back out. Why would it do such a thing? Maybe it was more like breathing? Perhaps it inhaled and exhaled the river in just the same way as he and the horse drew breath? It was a mystery he wished he could put before his father. Ashe would worry away at it until he had an answer. For now Oak had to set the question aside. He was thirsty. He drained the contents of his water vessel but it wasn't enough. It was not long now until sunset and he was parched.

If he filled his vessel from one of the rivulets before the rolling water overran it, that should be clean and safe to drink, shouldn't it? He jogged over the shingle towards the mud and then squelched through it, first ankle-deep, then knee-deep. It was unpleasant and it was hard going, but he must have water. Stopping at the first trickling stream, he scooped a handful to taste. Muddy, but fresh. He filled the boar's bladder and turned to go back.

The horse hadn't followed him onto the soft, sucking mud, but waited on the shingle. It was whickering, calling after him. The animal would need to drink too.

He carried the vessel to it, holding the neck wide so the horse could get its nose in. Once, twice, Oak refilled it and let the horse drink its fill and then he scooped more so he'd be able to quench his own thirst.

Muddy, cold and tired though he was, a sudden, extraordinary euphoria washed over him. He had survived a day in the river and now he had seen a place that no one in his clan knew existed, not even his father. He'd discovered the river's end. Seen the vast, rolling water. Looked across to the very edges of Mother Earth.

Ashe would be proud of him. He was always asking his son, "Why? Where? How?" Telling him, "Think, Oak! Think!" And Oak was at least starting to.

The sun was low in the sky now. He needed to find a safe place to sleep. At the foot of the shifting hillocks a great tree had been washed up. It was long dead, the bark seared off, the wood bleached in the sun and smoothed by the wind, but it gave some shelter from the breeze that came off the rolling water and it would be good to have something solid at his back. He ate what was left of the meat and berry mash in his pouch but it was barely sufficient to blunt the edge of his hunger. His stomach growled in protest and he remembered Willow on the return from the clan meet, handing him her food without a murmur. In his entire life he'd never ended the day without a full belly. He'd taken it as his due. *Stupid, selfish Oak!* His euphoria melted like mist.

He sat watching the waves edge up the beach, his mood growing darker as the light faded. The sinking sun turned the water first blood-red, then charcoal-black. As the night wrapped itself around him, the fears he'd pushed away in the light of day gathered like members of a hostile clan. For a moment he was in danger of being overwhelmed by them.

But then – as if it sensed what he was feeling – the horse lowered its head and blew a gentle, enquiring breath into his face. Oak blew back, a soft puff of breath into its nostrils.

"Don't worry," he said aloud. "We will get out of this. I *will* get you home, I promise."

The animal sank down beside him, warm and solid and alive. Oak moved close, leaning against its bulk. He had never been more grateful to a living creature than he was to the horse that night.

FISHING

The rolling water had ebbed by the time the sun rose. When he woke, Oak was pleased to see that the horse's wound was looking a lot better. There was no heat and no flies buzzed around it. As for him? The soreness of his hand was greatly reduced and the throbbing in his head had waned almost to nothing. He was, however, painfully hungry.

He walked away from the river's mouth, to where there were rocks covered with strange, slippery plants. Could any of those be edible? Dare he try? He cut a piece with his knife and nibbled cautiously. It had a strange, sharp tang but tasted pleasant enough. He swallowed, hoping that if it was bad, he'd vomit it back up quickly.

When he began to climb over the rocks, his

companion hung back. "Come on, Horse!" called Oak.

But Horse stayed on the shingle. Oak didn't like to leave him, but he had to find something to eat.

Between the rocks were pools left behind by the rolling water. Oak examined the strange things that lurked in them – was that a flower, or an animal? That thing that suckered down on the rock looked like a snail – could it be eaten?

He was about to prise it loose when he heard a sudden, desperate splashing to his heart side. At the same moment a great white bird swooped low over his head, screeching, trying to drive him away. There was something in the pool over there the bird wanted: it must be edible. He had to get to it first.

As he slithered across the rocks, scraping his legs, the bird swooped once, twice more. Oak flapped his arms to scare it away but the thing kept shrieking and diving at him. When he reached the pool, he saw something splashing that he assumed was a fish. It was so peculiar that if the bird hadn't been desperate to reach it, he wouldn't have dared eat the thing.

Grotesquely deformed, flat, with eyes on the top of its head, the fish had a mouth that had slipped sideways. With a prayer of thanks to the Goddess for this gift – however strangely shaped – Oak seized the thing by its tail. He muttered words of gratitude to the creature's spirit before giving it a flick and banging its head hard against the rock. Its blood spilled and its mouth stopped gaping open and shut. It was easier than he expected. The fish that swam in the river at home were slippery things, hard to catch and hard to keep hold of. They would shoot out of your hands if you squeezed them too tight. This felt rougher, coarser, with none of that slimy texture.

The bird hadn't given up. It dived at Oak's head again and again, trying to make him drop the fish as he returned across the rocks.

Horse greeted him with an excited whicker.

You're back! You're back!

"Yes," laughed Oak. "Did you miss me?"

Taking his knife, slitting open the fish's belly, Oak gutted it carefully. Then he threw head and entrails as far as he could across the rocks. The bird caught the head in mid-air and swallowed it down whole before pecking up the rest. It gave another cackling cry, a noise that sounded more like mocking laughter than thanks.

He should cook the fish, he supposed. But lighting a fire took so long and was so difficult. Although he had fire-stones in his pouch, he wasn't sure he had the skill to use them. Besides, he had neither cooking vessel nor sticks to hang it from.

So Oak ate the fish raw, slicing it into strips, wolfing them down almost without chewing. And then he cut more of the plant that grew on the rocks and ate until his belly stopped complaining.

Hunger finally satisfied, he turned his attention to the next problem: how to get home. Standing beside Horse, rubbing its neck absent-mindedly, Oak considered what little he knew of the land he was on.

The river flowed faster than a man could run and it had carried him for the length of a day. He'd then walked the length of a second to the rolling water. Rivers twisted and coiled back on themselves. They ran through ravines and chasms where no man could walk. It would certainly take more than two days to follow the river back to where he and Horse had plunged in. It might take as many as the fingers on both hands, possibly even more. He was fairly certain they wouldn't encounter any of the Bear clan while they were on the flat land close to the rolling water. He'd seen no signs of human habitation the day before, no charred remains of cooking fires, no tracks, no smoke, but when they left the flat, marshy plain – as they were bound to do – they would be trespassing on territory that the Bears *did* occupy. If he met any of them, what would happen?

Horse started to scratch Oak's shoulder with its teeth.

When they'd been carried in the river, Oak thought, and when they'd emerged onto that first little island, he'd been astride its back. It had been strange for both of them. Horses were prey animals. Meat, that was all. In all the fantastical traders' tales he'd listened to at clan meets, he'd never heard tell of a man doing what he'd done. Yet ... might it be possible to repeat the feat?

And if he did...?

Oak couldn't ask it to swim back across the river. As they'd walked the day before, he'd noticed Horse's terror of the swirling water. But if he could ride it the way he rode the bending beech branch at the clan meet, if it would carry him, if he could manage to stay on... Horse could move so much faster than him. They could travel swiftly together, go way upriver, past the place where they had first fallen in, high into the mountains where the river thinned to a stream. They could cross back to Deer land there and follow the river home.

And if they crossed paths with any Bears on the way? Oak recalled Horse on that first day, flowing over the grass with the speed of the wind and the smoothness of water. A thrilling thought tightened his throat. If he was on Horse, they could surely out-run any danger!

The shingle here crumbled underfoot. If he fell, it would be a relatively soft landing. Perhaps it was time to see if he could persuade Horse to let him sit on its back once more?

TRUSTING

Oak didn't know where to begin or how to start. He'd been carried on Horse's back in the river purely by accident and they'd both been equally scared and surprised by it. But maybe it was the will of the Goddess? Maybe this was what she'd intended all along?

How could he climb up without frightening the animal? One wrong move and he'd startle it. It might run away, and the thought of being on his own without Horse appalled him. So how could he persuade it that he meant no harm whilst trying to do something so odd?

As Oak turned the problem over, his father once more came to mind.

Trust.

That was what Ashe had said, when he'd been

trying to teach Oak about the qualities he'd need as chief. *The clan cannot survive unless each one trusts the others absolutely.*

It had been last summer, before he'd tamed Fang. They'd been watching the pack of dogs, Ashe laughing at the puppies playing in the dirt.

"Look at them," his father had said. One – maybe Fang? – had got over-excited and bitten the ear of the pack leader. It snarled a warning and the pup rolled onto its back at once, exposing its soft underbelly.

"Look," said Ashe. "See there? It's saying sorry. It's saying to the leader, *You can punish me if you like. You can rip me open. I won't stop you.* But it knows it's safe. It trusts its leader not to hurt it."

Did Horse trust him? Oak thought so. But how could he be sure? Was there some way to test it?

Horse was not like Fang. It was easy to know how a dog thought because they were so similar to people – a pack, working together for the common good, curious and excited about what might lie ahead. Yet Horse? Horse seemed constantly wary, constantly afraid. That was the crucial difference between predator and prey, Oak realized: where the hunter saw opportunity, the hunted saw only danger.

What was Horse's greatest weakness? What did it value above anything? Oak let his eyes run over

Horse's skin, trying to find a way into its head.

Horse had not followed him into the mud when he had filled his water vessel. It had not followed him onto the rocks, either.

Why?

Because it didn't want to go where the ground underfoot was treacherous. Being able to run, and run fast, was what kept it alive. If Horse injured its feet, its chances of survival would be impaired.

Horse would not roll over and expose its belly. But if it let Oak touch the soles of its feet? Yes ... then Oak would know the animal trusted him.

Horse was content. Leader was scratching itches he didn't know he had. Rump, back, belly, neck. Oh, this was good.

But then Leader's claws came down his shoulder, down his leg. He tensed. They closed around his ankle.

What was Leader doing?

Fight? Bite?

Snorting, he jerked away.

He eyed Leader. Leader's ears were not back; it was not squealing; its teeth were not bared. The noise it made was soft, soothing. But what was it doing?

Scratching again. Nice. Good.

But claws down leg again. Not good.

But not too bad.

Scratching. More scratching. Neck, face, chest.

Claws down leg again. Leader leaning, pushing his weight onto his other legs.

What does Leader want? Pick up hoof?

No!

Leader pulling, pulling gently.

Pick up hoof?

No!

Scratching, scratching, scratching. Down spine, over ribs.

Claws down leg.

Pick up hoof?

Leader is herd. Need herd. Need Leader.

At last! Horse lifted its hoof. Oak cupped it in his hands. It was not cleft into two distinct parts like that of deer or bison but was one solid whole, almost circular, hard as wood on the outside though the heel was soft and fleshy. After he'd held it for one, two breaths he gently passed the palm of one hand across its sole. The shingle that had been compacted fell away revealing an arrow-shaped part that pointed from heel to toe. When Oak touched it,

Horse's sides heaved; it snorted and tensed; but it did not snatch its hoof away.

"The Goddess must have marked your hoof like that when she made you," said Oak. "I wonder why…" It was almost like a sacred symbol.

Gently he set the hoof down. He stood for a few moments, overwhelmed at the great trust that had been placed in him. Responsibility settled on his shoulders, heavy as his father's bison-skin cloak, and as warm.

Praising Horse, rubbing its neck, Oak moved to the other side.

Having picked up one hoof, Oak thought it would be easier with the second. It was not. Horse was every bit as nervous and suspicious as it had been with the first. But the boy who had no patience for chipping arrowheads or practising his aim persisted. Scratching, rubbing, soothing Horse, Oak was barely aware of time passing. All his attention was on the animal, all that mattered was lifting that second hoof. And when he'd achieved it, he moved down Horse's spine to concentrate on his rear legs. He could feel Horse's alertness. There was a deep wariness there, but also an intense curiosity about what he might do next.

"Fearful and nosy," Oak said with a laugh. "That's

what you are, Horse. A very good combination."

Oak took the bow and quiver of arrows off his back. He untied his pouch, sheathed his knife and laid everything on the ground. He didn't want anything to swing or bang against Horse and cause it alarm. What Oak planned to do next would be surprising enough.

He turned all his attention on Horse, stroking it all over and humming until it seemed entirely relaxed. By then he was standing just behind Horse's shoulder again and their ribs were pressed together. Gently, slowly, he stretched both arms across its back, rubbing its other side, its flanks, with the palms of his hands. And then he jumped, up and forward so that he landed on his belly, draped across Horse's spine.

The animal was startled. It took a step forwards. It swayed sideways. It grunted in alarm and bunched its quarters ready for flight. But Oak kept up the soft, crooning noise and little by little Horse calmed itself. It stayed in place. It didn't throw Oak off and it didn't run.

Horse's head was up, neck stiff, but ears flicked back, listening to Oak.

What next? it seemed to ask. *What are you doing? What is this for?*

"Horse … I'm going to sit up now," Oak told it. "Stay still."

141

With painful slowness, twisting his top half towards Horse's head, pulling up one knee, Oak slid his foot across the animal's rump.

It was done. He was sitting on its back.

And Horse was letting him stay there.

The ground was a dizzyingly long way down. But how different the world looked from up here! How astonishing, to see the rolling water framed between the ears of a horse! This was surely a gift from the Goddess. With a heart full of gratitude, Oak thanked her.

At the corner of his eye, Oak caught a flutter of movement in the hillocks. He turned his head to look and Horse flicked an ear back, asking a question.

Over there?

Yes, Oak thought. *Let's go and see.*

Horse walked very slowly, feeling the strangeness of carrying weight on its back. Oak forced himself to breathe deeply, to keep every muscle relaxed.

The game he'd played riding the bending tree every year at the clan meet had served him well. He'd been terrible at it the first time, barely able to last more than a heartbeat before hitting the ground. Yew had laughed so much he'd have wet himself if Oak hadn't wiped the smile from his face with an angry slap. The memory brought a hot flush of shame now. There was no malice in Yew, Oak thought: the boy just liked to laugh and thought everything was a game. Whereas to him everything had always been a competition, a chance to prove his superiority. Oak had tried riding that branch again and again, forcing his friends to push the thing up and down and sideways long after they'd tired of it. He'd got hotter and crosser each time he'd fallen until they were all almost weeping with frustration. But at last he'd been so exhausted he stopped bracing himself against the tree's movement, stopped gripping so tightly with his legs. Instead, he'd become as soft and supple as the branch itself and that had made all the difference. He'd gone with the swaying: balancing, bending at the waist, staying with the branch each time it changed direction. Once he'd discovered the technique, he'd been able to outlast everyone else. And hadn't he let them know it? Glad though he was to have learned that skill, the thought of how he'd boasted made him squirm. If he ever got home, the first thing he'd do was say sorry to Yew and Lark.

As Horse walked towards the hillocks, Oak made no attempt to cling on with knees or calves. He did not grasp its neck hair for safety, much as he was tempted to. Instead, his hands were on Horse's shoulders, his fingers splayed either side of the stripe that ran the length of the animal's back. Oak tried to sit as lightly as if the creature was made of eggshell. He could scarcely believe it was real. Horse had obeyed his instruction!

No ... not instruction. Suggestion.

He wasn't master here, they were equals. Friends. Horse was clan.

RIDING

They had reached the place where the flat shingle ended and the line of hillocks began. Horse had barely started to climb the first when something burst from the reeds beneath its feet. Oak had the brief impression of something white flapping into Horse's face before the animal leaped sideways, turned tail and fled. Caught off guard, Oak was thrown, landing flat on his back. He lay winded and helpless, unable to move, gasping for breath.

They'd been attacked! The violence of Horse's reaction must mean the predator was large. Oak expected teeth or claws to rip his throat.

But then he saw it was only a bird, rising high into the sky now, circling him, cackling with the same mocking cry as the one to which he'd thrown the fish head.

Stupid Horse! Oak thought with a mixture of irritation and relief. How could a creature that size be scared of a bird?

Then he thought again. *No. Stupid Oak.* If he'd been looking at the world through Horse's eyes, he'd have anticipated that sudden leap. Horsekind survived by running from anything and everything that was even faintly alarming. If a horse paused to think, to look, to make sure – even for a heartbeat – it might be too late to flee. If Oak wanted to avoid being thrown again, he was going to have to see danger lurking behind every blade of grass the same way Horse did.

When the pain in his chest had subsided and he could breathe freely again, Oak got to his feet and walked across the shingle to where Horse stood, puffing and blowing. He stood beside it, scratching its neck, soothing it, telling it all was well, there was nothing to fear. And all the time he was thinking, *What next? What shall we do next?*

It was not the same as it had been when his father trained Fang. Ashe had worked with the creature's instincts, teaching the dog to go this way or that with a single wave of the hand. Before long, man and dog had seemed to think as one. And then, on the occasion Willow made such a magnificent kill, Fang ran with Ashe, herding the deer to the place where the hunters lay in wait. It had been remarkable. Wonderful, he supposed now, looking back on it. At the time he hadn't much liked Fang – it was so much his father's dog that it was overprotective, snarling if anyone went too near.

What had happened to Fang? Had the dog returned to its own kind? That last night of the clan meet when Oak had slipped away to go looking for his friends, had Fang abandoned Ashe too? Was that the last time he'd seen the dog? He recalled his father striding away across the plain after that dreadful fight with the Bear chief, flaming torch in hand. Alone. Whatever had happened to Fang must have happened that night…

Oak sighed. It was pointless brooding about it. He would discover the answers if he ever got home, and to make that journey he needed Horse. For now he must concentrate on the task he'd set himself.

He knew so little of horses! He'd only seen the herd that one morning before the world had turned upside down. Yet Horse was a grass-eater like deer or bison, constantly alert, picking up the slightest danger signal from others of its kind. In their herd of two, surely Horse would listen and watch anything Oak did? He'd already persuaded Horse to carry him towards the hillocks just by looking, by focusing his attention there and, he supposed, leaning slightly in that direction. Could he make it go anywhere he chose just by thinking clearly enough?

Slowly, gently, Oak got himself astride its back for a second time. He looked from the hillocks towards the rolling water. Stared at the waves.

There. Go there.

Horse's ears flicked, enquiring, back to him.

Yes, he thought, tilting a little forward, and obligingly Horse began to move.

But as they neared the water's edge Horse became nervous. Its hooves were sinking into wet, sucking shingle. Instead, Oak looked towards the distant river. *There.*

Relieved, Horse started to walk in the direction Oak had suggested.

But suppose he wanted to go faster?

Run! Oak thought, leaning forward. *Run!*

Danger?

No, said Oak. *Fun!*

Horse broke into the kind of jog that hunters use to cover great distances in a short time. It was every bit as bouncy as the tree branch had been. He couldn't help laughing for sheer joy and the sound made Horse change pace again. It lifted into a kind of floating run, faster, much faster, but smoother. It was easier than the jogging and Oak raised his arms in the air, whooping in delight at Horse's power and grace. Such speed! No wonder the Goddess had marked his hooves the way she had. Horse was fast as the flight of an arrow!

Oak felt that Horse could have run for ever: it was what the creature had been made for. But the mouth of the river was drawing near. How to stop him?

The boy stiffened his back. He stopped flexing with Horse's movement and instead resisted. It was so small a thing, so slight a sign, and yet it was enough to make Horse slow and then stop.

Weak-kneed, giddy with delight, Oak slid from the animal's back, exhilarated.

"Well done, clever, clever Horse!" He stroked and praised it for its bravery, he scratched its neck and Horse rubbed his shoulder with its teeth. And then the animal moved away, scraping the ground with one hoof and then another. Lowering its head, it sank to the ground and rolled this way and then the other, caking itself in shingle. Oak was bursting with joy and wonder. Horse was a divine gift; there could be no doubt whatsoever. The Goddess had preserved them both for this ... this miracle!

If they could do all this in just one morning – what else might they be capable of?

* * *

The sun was already high. Though Oak felt almost safe by the rolling water, there was little there for Horse to eat. It must be hungry and he was responsible for it now. He collected his weapons. Letting Horse see and smell them first, he slung his bow and arrows across his back and fastened his pouch and knife around his waist. Carefully, he re-mounted and then twisted so head and body were facing inland. *There*, he thought. *Go there.*

They left the shingle behind, Horse walking beside the river that would lead them home, snatching mouthfuls of dry, dusty grass on the way.

By mid-afternoon they'd reached the place where the plain met the marshy islands. He could see the willow tree where he'd sat the day before. Oak stopped for a moment. In the far distance to his knife-hand side was a smudge of dark green where the land rose into wooded hills. A cold fist squeezed his guts and his skin prickled into bumps. That was where the danger from the Bears would be at its greatest. It was difficult to judge, but he thought it was one, maybe two days away. He pushed his fears aside; he'd worry about them later, when he and Horse neared the forest.

The river glinted in the sunshine and with no mist to obscure it he could see its mainstream curved in a great arc that went way off to his heart side but then bent right back on itself. There was no need for them to follow its course exactly. If they cut straight across the plain, they would meet it over there without having to walk so far. And in between here and there was a small copse of trees and a line of bright green grass that suggested a stream flowed there. Horse would be able to eat well that night, Oak thought, even if he went hungry. If they could reach it before sunset, it would be the perfect place to make camp.

FLYING

Oak woke at dawn knowing that something was terribly wrong.

He lay on his back looking up at the sky through the tree he'd slept under. Its leaves quivered as if in a breeze, yet the air was still. He could hear a faint rumbling that seemed to echo in his guts.

Was it thunder? Were the rains finally coming?

No ... the sky was clear, cloudless. And the noise did not swell and fade like thunderclaps but carried on growing steadily louder.

He could feel through his back that the ground itself was pulsing.

Horse, an uneaten clump of grass swinging between its teeth, raised its head and sniffed the air, nostrils wide with alarm. It emptied its bowels, ready for flight.

Run! Run!

Oak caught the animal's panic. Seizing his weapons, he scrambled to his feet. The day was exceptionally clear. Oak could see further across the grassy plain than he'd been able to the day before. There, in the far distance, were hills, smudged dark green by the beginnings of the forest, behind them the high mountains. But in front, on the flat land, rapidly obscuring both hill and mountain rose a great billowing cloud.

Coming closer with each heartbeat.

Smoke? No ... there were no flames, no crackle of fire, only this pounding that was making the ground beneath his feet tremble and setting his teeth jangling. His stomach clenched.

What was it?

Not smoke. Dust.

Dry earth, kicked up by many, many hooves. A dark stain of flesh, spreading across the plain like a flood.

Oh dear Goddess! Aurochs! Twice as large, twice as heavy as Horse and with horns as long as Oak's arm. He had seen with his own eyes the damage those horns could do. Beech, slashed from groin to chest, guts spilling out, dying in screaming agony and nothing anyone – even Rowan – could do to save him.

The herd was on the move because of the drought, seeking fresh grass but not walking slowly with their young as they normally would. Stampeding. Something had frightened them and now a torrent of horned creatures was pouring towards Oak and Horse. Aurochs were bellowing, calling to each other, screaming, *Danger! Danger!*

Oak didn't stop to think about what had set them running.

Where could he and Horse go? What could they do? The herd had spread so far across the plain there was no way of evading it. They would be swept away in the flood.

Could they outrun them? They had to!

The day before, Oak had approached Horse gently, giving the animal time to become accustomed to his weight. But every moment the herd drew closer. Horse had caught the scent of whatever was driving the aurochs towards them and was terrified. Eyes rolling, nostrils flaring, it squealed with fright.

But the animal stood its ground. Because Oak had not yet told it to run.

Though weakened by hunger, terror now gave Oak's legs and arms the strength for him to vault onto Horse's back.

The herd was almost upon them.

Go!

Horse flew into a run from a standstill. For one breath, maybe two, they were ahead of the herd. But then the leaders caught up and overtook. Horse and boy were surrounded by great horned beasts, heaving flanks and hot walls of muscle hemming them in on either side.

But Horse was a prey animal, like them. Herd. The aurochs would not harm Horse if they could avoid it. And as long as Oak stayed on its back he too would be safe.

Oak made no attempt to direct Horse. The animal understood the nature of a stampeding herd in a way that he could not. Horse must find its own path. All Oak's attention was on staying astride its back. If he lost his balance, if he slipped and fell, he would be trampled to a bloody pulp before he could draw breath to scream.

Herd running.
Running to Galloping Water.
No. NO!

Scared. Scared. Scared.

Oak, seeing through Horse's eyes, looked with horror at the river ahead. There was no way of escaping the tide of flesh carrying them along. They would have to enter the water, and with so many thrashing legs, so many pointed horns, surely they could not survive.

But wait, the herd leaders were changing direction, trying to find the easiest way into the water. Oak and Horse were still running with the herd but there were fewer animals to Oak's heart side than there had been. Yet still, there was no way out.

Until one tripped.

It was running so fast it carried on moving forward, crashing into the calf ahead, bringing it down. The calf screamed, and its mother whirled around to protect her young. Aurochs stopped, turned, twisted, sweeping one way or the other to avoid trampling the fallen calf.

And for one fraction of a moment there was a gap wide enough for Horse to pass through.

Yes?

Yes! said Oak.

Turn. Dodge. Jump!

Horse gathered itself and in one mighty leap soared over the fallen calf.

Free!

The herd moved on.

Boy and horse were left behind.

Dust thick in their throats, coughing, wheezing, hearts pounding, Oak and Horse watched the last aurochs plunge into the river and strike out across it.

Weak with relief, hardly able to believe what had just happened, Oak slumped forward and wrapped his arms around Horse's neck. They'd been airborne. Actually airborne. Horse had flown and carried him with it. For one dizzying moment he'd known what it was to be a bird.

FIGHTING

Awash with so many emotions he couldn't even put a name to, Oak took longer than he should have to sense Horse's thoughts.

Danger!

Oak sat up. And saw why the herd had been stampeding.

The aurochs had fled. But now he and Horse were surrounded by wolves.

The pack could not believe its luck. Out of that vast herd had come an animal with no horns. Smaller. Less meat on it. But easier – far easier – to kill. And they were tired now, hungry and desperate for blood.

Yet there was something strange about this

creature. It looked like horse, smelled like horse, but from its back grew a strange man-like parasite that snarled and growled and bared its teeth at them.

Horse or man on their own were easy prey. But this strange combination of the two was alarming. Wrong.

And so the wolves hung back.

Oak was fired by the savage joy of having survived the stampede, of having stayed on Horse's back through that wild flight. He hadn't slipped, not even when Horse made that desperate leap across the fallen calf! He was so grateful to Horse for keeping them both alive and unharmed, that now – facing a new threat – his temper exploded.

Rage conquered fear. He did not cower before the wolves. Instead he yelled and screamed at the pack, and when they did not at once attack he had the wit to pull the bow from his back and fit an arrow to the string.

Which is the leader? he thought fiercely. *That one.*

Without hesitation, Oak fired.

He missed.

Of course he did. He hadn't eaten since the previous morning and the surge of terrified energy that had propelled him onto Horse's back and kept him clinging there during the stampede was rapidly ebbing.

His hands shook as he fired the arrow, so rather than plunging into the lead wolf's neck, it merely clipped its ear and then thudded into the dirt.

But that sting of pain was enough.

It may have simply been the arrow. Oak later admitted to himself that it was lucky that an aurochs – maybe the one that had tripped into the calf – was hurt. Though it had got back on its feet and entered the water, it had not swum across with the rest but was mired in the mud of the ebbing river.

Prey that was injured and weakened was better than prey that was strange and peculiar and that yelled and screamed and fought back.

The leader of the wolf pack barked a command. The other wolves flowed over the mud towards the hapless aurochs.

Go! Oak thought.

Where?

Away. Fast.

The air became thick with snarling and snapping and the bellowing of an animal facing an agonizing death. The kill would not be quick and it would not be clean. Neither Oak nor Horse wanted to hear it.

Horse was tired and shaken. But it turned its back

on the dreadful scene and, breaking into a jog, kept moving until boy and horse were out of sight and sound of the wolves.

THINKING

Horse slowed to a walk. Oak slumped on its back, faint with hunger. He had to find food. The smudge of forest in the distance seemed no closer, and he would need all his wits about him in another day or two when they reached it. He should stop here on the plain where he was relatively safe, he thought. Maybe he could spear a fish in the river? Or could he throw a stone and bring down one of those birds that waded in the mud?

Oak was wondering what he should attempt first when he caught sight of a young hare. Small, solitary, it lolloped a few paces, crossing their path, and then sat down in the grass. Turning its head, it looked back at Horse and Oak in confusion.

It was considering flight, but there was no smell of

predator. Oak's scent was entirely masked by Horse's. Grass. Dung. Sweat. Whatever the thing was, the hare decided, it must be herbivore, like himself. Prey, not predator. The two-headed creature was odd, but there was nothing to fear.

Slowly Oak reached for an arrow. He focused on the hare, and Horse walked towards it.

They were practically on top of the animal. Though a poor shot, Oak could not miss. The hare was dead before it knew it was in danger.

It had given its life to preserve Oak's. He thanked it, saying the words that would free its soul to run in the spirit world. He gave thanks to the Goddess who had put the hare in his path. And then he set about butchering it. He'd seen it done so many times, and yet had never performed the task himself. Taking his knife to the fur, wincing at the unpleasantness of it, he slit open the belly. Its guts spilled free, a slippery bloody mess. Clumsily he cut loose the heart, the kidneys, the liver, then stripped the guts and stretched them out to dry. There would be plenty of use for those later, as thread to sew with, or as twine to bind an arrowhead to a shaft, if only he could remember how. He skinned the animal as best he could, his mouth watering in anticipation of its roasted flesh.

But first he had to try and make a fire.

He pictured Willow kneeling, striking fire-stones onto a pile of dry leaves, blowing the sparks into flames, feeding the fire with twigs until it caught. She always made it look so easy. And so would he. Eventually. If the Goddess guided him home, he'd work at it until he'd mastered the skill. One day, he swore, he would kill and cook a meal for his sister.

Oak gathered what he needed: dry grass for kindling. Handfuls of small twigs. A few larger ones to feed the fire once it had taken. And then he fished the fire-stones from his pouch. He hardly knew how to hold them and his hands were shaking after the rigours of the morning. He struck the stones together. Nothing. He adjusted his grip. Tried again. Still nothing. Again. Again. Sweat ran from his forehead and trickled between his shoulder blades but Oak was determined to succeed. And at last – when he was near to weeping with frustration – a spark fell onto the pile of dried grass. It flared and died before he could lower his face to feed it with his breath, but he had the knack now. He struck the stones in rapid succession once, twice, many times, then blew gently, praying all the while that those tiny dots of red would grow into flames.

It had taken Oak twice as long as Willow to make a fire half the size, but he had done it. Goddess be praised!

Stacking stones either side, he skewered the hare's carcass and organs onto the arrow that had killed it, and suspended it over the flames. While it cooked, he attempted to cure the skin the way he'd seen his sister do so often. He could make something from the hare's hide later, perhaps, if his clumsiness hadn't made the thing useless.

Cooking was not as simple as it looked. The hare was charred on the outside, raw and bloody in the middle, but Oak was so hungry by then he didn't care. He forced himself to eat slowly. It would have been easy to gobble down the whole animal but he was well aware he should keep something in reserve. Once he'd blunted the sharpness of his hunger, he cut the bloody meat off the bones and laid it on a stone, which he set in the embers of the dying fire. It would dry, he hoped, and then he could store it in his pouch.

He sat, watching it while Horse cropped the grass near by. He doubted it would be enough meat to get him home, but if he needed to hunt again, he knew now that it was easier on Horse. The hare had not even tried to run away.

Oak thought over the morning's events. The stampede had been astonishing, terrifying, but thrilling too. Horse had been part of the herd, flowing in and out, weaving between the animals, knowing their minds, thinking their thoughts.

And then the wolves – who had held them at bay – had not attacked. They had been so confused by the sight of a boy on a horse that they'd been easy to drive off.

Nothing happened without reason, Rowan said. All this must be for some purpose. Horse had already saved his life so many times in so many ways! The hand of the Goddess was at work here; she was preserving him – but for what? He felt her nudging him towards something. Rowan had predicted at his birth that the clan's fortunes would rise with him. How arrogant that prophecy had made him! He'd thought himself so very special. He'd believed that all he'd need to do as chief was stride around and let people admire him. Idiot!

Well, he'd learned his lesson now. The Goddess wanted him to do something, and humbly he would do her will, if he could only discover what it was.

It felt to Oak as though the Goddess was standing, arms folded, beside him, muttering the words of his father: *Think, Oak. Think.*

Oak thought of his clan. Images flashed through his head. Thorn, injured. Beech, dead. Why? Because it was so hard to bring down a large animal: it took as many hunters as the fingers on both hands, and they were often desperately hurt. The chase was so dangerous, a hunter risked being trampled, bitten, kicked: there were so many ways prey could fight back.

And yet he had ridden in amongst a herd of aurochs and survived without so much as a bruise.

The thought came like a whisper, surely from the mouth of the Goddess. Suppose he were to ride Horse into a herd of quietly grazing deer? Would they run, or would they ignore him? Could it be done? Could he get close enough to kill with a single arrow? A single spear?

Not yet. In all honesty, he knew that even if he practised every waking moment, it would be a long time before he had Willow's or his father's skill with a weapon! And even then, a lone hunter in a herd would be so vulnerable.

But suppose what he'd done with Horse could be copied by other members of the clan? Was such a thing possible?

Hunters, on horses...?

His heart raced. A world of new possibilities opened before him, setting his mind ablaze.

He thought of the journey from the clan meet – how long it had taken, how hard it had been for young and old alike. But what if they were all riding?

Images unfolded in his head. Was this what the

Goddess intended? Or was it just a silly, childish fancy? Impossible and unnatural.

Unnatural.

A sudden recollection of the chiefs dropped into his mind: the clan meet, when they'd talked of the drought and what had caused it. Oak's attention had been wandering far and wide until Roc, the Bear leader had said loudly, "It's unnatural!"

He'd been glaring at Ashe. Fang had growled as the dog often did when it thought its master was being threatened.

Then Roc had said, "The Goddess ordained how we should live. Her rules should not be broken."

Ashe had laid a hand on Fang's head to quiet the dog and then said gently, "You think nothing should change. But why did the Goddess give us brains to think if she did not mean us to use them?"

Oak hadn't understood the exchange at the time and he didn't now. He'd paid little heed because it was well known that Ashe and Roc disagreed at every clan meet. The elders joked about it, laying bets as to what they would fall out over this time. When Ashe first built a shelter that was rooted to the ground, Roc told him it was unnatural. He said a clan was not meant to settle in one place but to roam wherever the Goddess willed. He told Ashe that he was violating the spirit of the trees by bending them to his will. And then, the following year when Ashe had cleared a circle of land and planted seeds, Roc said it would offend the Goddess: it was for her to decide where things did or didn't grow. Their disagreements had always been amicable enough, any ill temper washed away by the mead as the drinking horn was passed from mouth to mouth.

Until that last meet, when the two chiefs had fought and the two clans had become deadly enemies.

Oak wondered again what had happened to Fang that night. But it was a puzzle he couldn't solve yet. His mind turned back to horses. He had a brain; he would use it. Ashe had devised a way of teaching Fang to work with him. Could Oak do the same, not just with Horse, but with others? Might it be possible to capture a whole herd? To tame and train not one, but many? How could it be done?

His mind buzzed with ideas.

Oak was so absorbed in his thoughts, he didn't hear Horse's snort of alarm or the stamp of warning.

So it came as a shock to look up and find a spear pointing at his throat.

PART III
HORSE BOY

CAPTIVE

The blade was not the grey-black flint favoured by the Deer clan but white bone, long and barbed so it could not easily be pulled out of the flesh.

The man holding it glared at Oak with suspicion, hatred and – was it possible? – fear.

Why fear?

The necklace of teeth around his neck, the carved totem dangling at the end of it, marked this man as one of the Bear people. There was something familiar about his wide, flat nose and high cheekbones. Oak had paid little attention at the clan gathering, but he thought maybe this man had been standing beside Roc, the Bear chief, when he addressed the other leaders. Was this his son?

He was not alone.

There were as many of them as the fingers on one hand. Young, but still older than Oak. Taller, bigger, stronger. Yet all looking afraid. One glanced nervously up at the vast sky as if – without trees to hold it up – he thought it might fall on them. Ashe was right about them feeling naked without a canopy of leaves to protect them. They didn't like being out on an open plain. Why were they here?

The urge to run was overwhelming. Oak could duck under their arms, scramble onto Horse, gallop away. But even as the idea crossed his mind, he dismissed it. That barbed spear would pierce his back long before he'd reached the animal. At least his death would be relatively quick. But what might they do to Horse afterwards? To them, it was prey. Prey lived only to be killed. Eaten. The thought made Oak's stomach heave.

"Get up," said the man. "You're to come with us."

They took his knife, his bow, his arrows, his pouch and water vessel. They bound his wrists behind his back.

"What should we do with that?" asked another man, nodding towards Horse.

"Alder said to leave it alone," replied the man, looking at Oak's companion as if Horse were a leech or a tick. "It will decide its own fate."

The Bears helped themselves to the remains of the hare Oak had set drying in the fire.

And then, pointing their spears at his back, they forced Oak to start walking.

Things with pointed sticks. Smell of fear.
Danger? Run?
No... Leader is leading. Like stallion of herd.
Things walk behind.
Follow?
Follow.

They walked until the sun was high overhead, Oak simmering with rage. He'd let his guard slip! He'd so lost himself in thoughts of a glorious future, he'd forgotten the present danger. He'd even lit a cooking fire. Idiot! The smoke must have been like a signal to the enemy clan. But how, Oak thought, had they seen it? He had still been a great distance from the forest: why had they ventured so far from the trees? It was almost as if they had been looking for signs of his arrival. Why? How had they even known he was their side of the river, lost and unwillingly trespassing on their land?

When the little group stopped to rest, to eat and drink, the Bears kept Oak tightly surrounded. Horse grazed some distance away, out of reach of their spears.

"It's following, then," said one of the men. There was revulsion in his voice.

"Yes," replied the younger man, who might be the chief's son. He added something under his breath. It was spoken so softly that Oak could not be sure, but he thought it was that word again: *unnatural*.

Why did Horse bother them so much? Half of him wished the creature would run and find its way back to the herd. But the other half needed it to stay. As long as Horse was here, he was not alone. Strange, to feel more fellowship with an animal than these wild, angry men!

Oak was allowed to eat a strip of meat and drink from the water vessel they held to his lips. The Bears stared at him so hard it was difficult to swallow and the food tasted like dung in his mouth.

Fear tightened Oak's throat and made speaking an effort, but he forced himself to ask, "Why have you taken me captive?"

"Roc's orders," snapped the man who kept glancing up at the sky. "We've been told to bring you to the chief, that's all."

"What will he do to me?"

"That's for my father to decide."

So the younger man *was* Roc's son then. A son didn't always succeed his father as leader, but if he was chief-in-waiting it would give them something in common. Oak could use that somehow, couldn't he?

"I've done nothing to you," Oak said. "Neither has Horse."

Son of Roc bent down so his face was a finger's width from Oak's. Very softly, very quietly, in a voice icy with menace, he said, "Shut your mouth or I'll shut it for you. Not another word, or by the time we get you back to camp you'll have lost your tongue."

Oak didn't doubt the sincerity of the threat. The thought of having his tongue sliced from his head made him feel so sick he could barely keep the meat he'd swallowed down in his stomach. When they set off again, it took all his strength to simply put one foot in front of the other.

His mind was in turmoil. How had things come to this? For a man – a chief's son – to threaten a boy, a child from another clan, was unheard of. Unimaginable. Like something out of a fireside tale. And yet that was exactly what had just happened. Why had everything in the world gone so badly off-kilter? How could the Goddess allow it?

Think, Oak. Think. The Goddess gave you a brain. Use it.

Think. Remember.

All of these men must have been at the clan gathering. He'd have camped alongside them. They'd have been there at the sacred ritual, at the chiefs' meetings, the final feast.

Oak stole a glance at them. Yes ... if he remembered that last meal rightly, he knew where each of them had sat. Roc's son, beside his father. That one had been to his knife-hand side, the other at his back. That one had snatched at the mead horn and drunk so deep he'd vomited not long after.

But that one – that one with the sharply pointed, beak-like nose and mass of hair – he'd not been there. Why?

Oak remembered his sister sitting beside a man on the bending branch. Was this who she'd crept off to meet? Oak had thrown a stone just as they'd been about to kiss, and Willow had exploded with rage. It was a shaming memory to recall.

Goddess! Let me live long enough to say sorry! Let her be alive to hear me.

Once again images came in lightning flashes. Willow's blood, misting the air. The crack of teeth snapping shut. At least he *hoped* it was her teeth, and not her jawbone breaking. Broken bones took so long to heal. And a jaw? How would she eat? Whatever her injuries, he hoped no sickness had come afterwards. He'd known hunters who'd died not from their wounds but from the fever that often followed.

"Goddess, preserve Willow!"

He didn't realize he'd spoken aloud until he felt the prod of a spear at his back. He stumbled and quickly righted himself. Then he stole a small glance over his shoulder.

"I said, shut your mouth. Not a word. Not even in prayer."

Roc's son looked as surly as ever. The jaw of the beak-nosed-man was clenched tight, but he could not disguise the fire that now burned in his eyes. Was that because Oak had mentioned Willow's name? For the first time since his capture, Oak felt a faint fluttering of hope.

LISTENING

It was as Oak thought: they were more than a day's walk from the forest. Camp that night was made beside the river, where the land was flat and the air full of mosquitoes. The Bears lit a cooking fire and kept it burning long after they had eaten in the hope the smoke would drive the insects away. They sat around it, slapping and scratching irritably.

Horse, equally troubled by biting flies, stood some way off, swishing its tail, stamping its feet and tossing its head. Every so often its entire body shuddered with irritation. Oak could feel the animal wanting to come closer to him for safety's sake but fearing the Bears. He wished he could go over to talk to Horse, to squash the mosquitoes that ravaged it, to put his arms around its neck and feel its warmth.

When he thought of what might lie ahead, Oak's stomach tightened. In the darkness his imagination conjured all kinds of horrors. Questions banged around inside his skull, making his head ache. Why were they doing this? What did they even want with him? He didn't know what had happened between Ashe and Roc but he knew that a son shouldn't be punished for his father's actions. Oak was on the cusp of manhood but he was still counted as a child, and children of any clan were to be treated kindly by their elders. It was part of the accepted codes of behaviour: the clans' rules, the natural law.

The natural law. That Roc seemed to suggest Ashe had broken.

Unnatural.

Oak didn't dare speak, but he could listen. Perhaps he'd learn more that way.

Once he'd eaten, Oak yawned, rubbed his eyes and drooped, seemingly with exhaustion.

His captors were taking no chances. Roc's son tied Oak's wrists and ankles together so he couldn't run away. Miserably, he lay on his side and pretended to sleep, letting his limbs relax, slowing his breathing, twitching and mumbling occasionally as if dreaming.

It wasn't long before the Bears started talking.

And as Oak lay there, that faint fluttering of hope grew. Though the Bears had seemed united against him, there was one who was evidently uneasy about whatever was planned.

The man had said so little, spoken so infrequently, that Oak couldn't identify the voice. He didn't dare open his eyes to see which of them was speaking but he hoped it was the hooked-nose man whose eyes had burned at the mention of Willow.

"Is this him, then? The Changer. Really?"

The man who replied was defensive. Roc's son, Oak thought, though he couldn't be sure. "Yes."

"He's a child, Birra!"

Birra. So that's the name of the chief's son. Remember that, Oak.

"So?" Birra said irritably.

"Look at him! How could he be responsible for the drought?"

"The horse is following him. What more proof do you want?" Birra's tone was icy. Dangerous. "They both say it's him. Would you doubt their word?"

The speaker clearly did. "Alder swore it was his father's fault only one moon ago."

Alder? He'd heard that name before. Where? When?

"It was reasonable enough to think so."

The doubter gave a sceptical grunt.

"Why are you so reluctant to believe?" Birra asked. He laughed mockingly. "It's because of the girl, isn't it. What was her name? Willow? Yes, Fin, I saw you sneaking off after her. She got right under your skin, didn't she? And now you doubt the sage's wisdom?"

Ah! So Oak was right. Beak Nose was Willow's friend. He was called Fin, and he was angry now.

"Roc did his bidding," said Fin. "And what a bloody mess that was! I bet he never thought a dog could put up such a fight. Nearly got his throat torn out. And for what? It didn't end the drought, did it?"

"No, it didn't. Because the dog was not the only cause!" Birra was clearly furious. If he'd shouted and raged, he would have been less terrifying, but his voice became deathly quiet and so cold that Oak began to shiver. "Your judgement is blurred by your love for the boy's sister. Put her out of your head. The Goddess had not revealed everything at the clan meet. It was easy to misread the signs. But this time the sage is certain. And so is my father. We will do whatever is required to end this drought. If you don't like it – well, you can choose to be outcast."

Outcast. That word again, from the fabled savage times that should have no place in the real, living world.

There was a long silence. And then any fleeting

hope of Oak finding an ally amongst the Bears vanished.

"I must bow to my chief's wisdom," said Fin finally. "And the sage's." With that, Willow's admirer fell silent.

For several heartbeats there was only the crackling of the fire, the flow of the river, the whine of mosquitoes and the men scratching.

Then Fin asked, "What will happen to the boy?"

"He will be dealt with."

"And the horse?"

"Same as the dog. Beasts must keep to their own kind; it is what the Goddess has decreed. Creatures that allow themselves to be bent to the will of man anger our Mother Earth. If they break her rules, they must pay the price."

No more was said. But Oak had the answer to Willow's question. He knew what had happened to Fang.

For reasons he couldn't begin to comprehend, the Bears had killed his father's dog.

They planned to do the same to Horse.

And to him?

FOREST

Though the wooded hills stretched as far as the river, the Bear clan's camp must be in a different, distant part of the forest, Oak thought, because the following day they turned their backs on the river he'd hoped would lead him home and cut across the flat land. Oak's limbs felt heavy. The ties chafed against his wrists. Sick with fear, he had slept little, his mind running in circles, trying to think of a means of escape.

He'd come up with nothing. Nothing at all.

When they prodded him, he moved. When they fed him, he chewed. When they held a water vessel to his lips, he drank. What else could he do?

Horse followed all day but became increasingly anxious as the group neared the trees.

Where are we going? Where? Where? Why?

Horse must run away, thought Oak. It would be dangerous for the creature to be alone on the plain, but it would stand more chance against a pack of wolves than the assembled Bear clan.

How could he tell Horse that? How could he explain that people who looked like Oak, sounded like him, smelled like him, were not herd, but enemies? That they meant to do harm to Horse? To them both?

Go, he thought. *Run. Get away.*

Where? Where? Why?

By the time they reached the beginning of the forest, Horse was hanging further back. The tie that bound them had stretched. It would snap soon, thought Oak. Horse would run and leave him to his fate.

Not trees. Danger! Wolves hiding. Lynx stalking. Bear hunting.
Can't run through trees.
Come back, Leader!
Danger! Danger!!!
Stop!

186

Bad leader. Bad.

"What's wrong with it?" said Birra.

Oak looked back at Horse.

It was prancing this way and that, showing itself off. Stamping a furious warning, whinnying.

He'd seen Horse behave that way before. It had baffled him then, but he knew Horse now; he understood what it was thinking.

Scared!

Of course you are.

Don't go there!

Got to.

Bad Leader.

Horse was challenging him. Telling Oak he was doing the wrong thing. Offering to take his place as leader if Oak would only follow.

"Call it," snapped Birra. "Make it come."

"What?" said Oak. Out of the corner of his eye he saw a flicker of discomfort cross Fin's face.

"Make it come," Birra repeated. "Or we kill it here."

It was an empty threat, Oak thought. If they tried attacking Horse in the open, it would gallop out of reach of their spears before they'd even thrown them. And they wouldn't want to risk losing their human captive by turning their attention to the animal.

Birra prodded Oak so hard with his spear he punctured skin. Oak barely noticed.

Ashe's words were running through his mind: *Staring any animal straight in the eyes is a challenge. It will drive it away.*

Oak fixed his eyes on the horse and took a step towards it. Horse, unnerved, did exactly what he'd hoped, and backed off.

"Come on," Oak called. "Come here." He stared and stared, his eyes and body giving Horse the opposite message to the words that came out of his mouth.

"Come along now," he said, like a mother talking to a young child. "We've got to go into the forest."

He took another step forward and Horse wheeled around, jogging even further from the trees.

Run, Horse! he thought. *Get away. Find herd. Be safe.*

Behind him he heard Fin say, "He can't control that animal. Are you sure he's the cause?"

"It is for the sage to decide," Birra snapped. "We

take him to Alder as we have sworn to do. It is the will of the Goddess! We can hunt that thing down later if we need to."

Pushing Oak ahead of them, the Bears entered the trees.

Horse hung back.

Wolves behind. Trees ahead.
Stop! Stop! Come back!

Go! thought Oak. *Run.*

He could hear Horse's short, heavy breaths, fearful snorts, angry stamp. It gave one last, desperate, screaming whinny.

Stop!!!

And then – just as Oak was sure the animal would turn tail and flee across the plain – Horse burst into the forest, trampling through the tinder-dry undergrowth, breaking branches in its haste to catch up with Oak. The creature was as loyal to him as Fang had been to his father. Horse would not, could not, go anywhere without him.

Oak felt his heart snap in two.

BETRAYAL

In the thick forest Oak could not see the passage of the sun overhead and lost all sense of time. Though he tried to memorize landmarks, to fix the path in his mind, one tree looked so much like another that it was a futile task. If he escaped, he'd no doubt run in a circle straight back into the arms of his captors.

Horse, spooked by every cracking branch and tugging thorn, kept so close to Oak he could feel its breath on his skin. It made Birra more bad-tempered than ever but there was little he could do to prevent it.

The air grew hotter and heavier. The canopy was dense, casting such deep shadows it was difficult for Oak to see where to set his feet, but in places blindingly bright shafts of light sliced through making his head ache. Though Oak's brain turned and twisted, searching for shreds of opportunity for escape, he found none.

It was almost dark when the smell of cooking fires wreathed between the scents of pine and fern. It should have been comforting, thought Oak. It should have meant rest and food and company. Instead it reeked of danger.

The group pushed onwards, weaving between trees, around bushes of briar and through patches of nettle towards a slight rise in the land.

When they crested it Oak saw a clearing and a camp spread out below. Shock stroked a cold finger down his spine.

He knew that the Bears – like every clan except Deer – lived as nomads, moving from place to place, sheltering beneath bushes or in caves. They lived lightly, leaving no trace of their passing. They took only the prey the Goddess saw fit to send across their path, and though they gathered the fruit she hung from bushes, they did not plant their own seeds. And they never, ever cut down a tree, for where would its spirit live?

But now the Bears had broken their own taboo. The clearing was a natural one – it was evident to Oak that a great pine had come down some time ago and smashed a hole in the forest as it fell. There at the centre, two new trees had sprung up to take its place. But they had been maimed, lower branches ripped away so the trunks were straight and smooth as the stakes that stood at the middle of the stone temple on the sacred plain.

The spear was pressed against Oak's back once again.

"Move!" barked Birra.

He had no choice. Oak started the descent to the camp and Horse followed.

Those tending the cooking fires fell silent as the group approached. Even the smallest baby's cry died in its throat. Oak's eyes darted from face to face. Everyone stared. All of them were fearful. Angry, even. There were children that Oak recognized from the clan gatherings, those he'd raced and played with, now glaring at him with eyes full of hate. He'd get no help from any of them.

Roc, the Bear chief, emerged from the shadows. He looked at Oak and Horse, teeth bared like a wolf. There was a scar running from below one ear and across his throat, a ragged line of purple, the skin flaming red either side. Fang had left his mark, then. Good.

Beside Roc stood a man marked with tattoos and dripping with totems. This must be Alder, the clan's sage. Revulsion rose from him like a heat haze. Fear squeezed Oak's throat.

What ghastly vision had the Goddess shown the sage that made him look at Oak like that?

Then – from somewhere behind him – Oak heard a familiar voice. A woman's. Turning, he saw Rowan.

Rowan! Seer of what has been and what is to come; healer, whose gentle hands smoothed the coming of souls into the world and eased their passing from it; sage, senior and most revered member of the Deer clan. Rowan, who everyone turned to in times of trouble, who had foretold at his birth that his people's fortunes would rise with him.

He'd never been more delighted to see anyone. But what in the name of the Goddess was she doing here?

"Put down your weapons," Rowan instructed the men. "There is no need of them." And at once the Bears' spears were lowered.

She came towards Oak, arms open. Oak ran to her and was enfolded in her warm embrace.

Oak breathed in her scent – mountain air, rushing streams and fresh-sprung grass, deer meat roasting with juniper and thyme. The smell of home overwhelmed him. All at once Oak was a child again. Rowan was so old, so wise. She would make all his troubles disappear.

"You must do what I tell you," she said, pushing him away gently.

Oak nodded, heart thumping.

"I will put everything right," she promised.

Taking her knife in her gnarled hand, Rowan cut the ties that bound Oak's wrists. Then she picked up a length of plaited hide and gave it to Oak. "There is something that must be done. Can you get this around the animal's neck?"

Oak was surprised. "Why?" he blurted.

The sage was not used to being questioned. She gave him a warning look but answered, "So we can lead it home."

A whisper of suspicion stirred deep in Oak's belly. She was all-seeing, wasn't she? Didn't she know there was no need? Didn't she realize that Horse would follow him anywhere? But of course, they were surrounded by enemies. Though the spears' points were lowered, the Bears still clutched the hafts tightly in their hands. Perhaps Rowan thought it best not to remind them of the power Oak had over the creature.

Oak took the rope and approached Horse. He rubbed its neck, scratching down into the hair, finding the spot it liked best. He let the animal nuzzle him back, nibble his shoulder, felt Horse relax a little. This was comfortable. This was familiar. This was herd.

Oak held the rope so Horse could sniff it. Ran the thing over its shoulder, letting the animal get used to the feel of it before he slid it over its ears and down its neck.

"This one, too." Rowan had a second in her hand.

The whisper of suspicion grew more distinct. But Rowan was of the Deer clan. Oak obeyed.

And because Oak had placed the ropes around his neck, Horse did not struggle.

Rowan walked over to the boy and the horse.

The Deer sage raised her hand and the Bear clan seized the ropes – more men than the fingers on both Oak's hands. And then Roc's strong arms were around Oak, holding a knife to his throat while his son tied his wrists once more. Rowan stood and watched.

The Bear men tried to force Horse towards the two stripped tree trunks at the middle of the clearing. Oak knew that had the men walked calmly ahead, had they not turned back, had they not stared into its eyes, the animal might, possibly, have been led by them.

But when they looked at the horse, it saw its own fear reflected in their eyes. They were not to be trusted. Horse resisted. The ropes tightened around its neck.

Horse screamed and kicked, but it was being choked by hide ropes. The ropes Oak himself had put there.

Now Oak was screaming too.

There was more than fear and rage in Horse's panicked cries.

There was confusion. Sadness.

Betrayal.

Why? Why?

The pain was beyond bearing. Oak was so ashamed, that when Rowan held a cup to his lips and told him to drink, he did not struggle. Oak tasted something sharp and bitter and wondered if it was poison. He had a brief recollection of Rowan holding the mead horn out to his father at the clan gathering's final feast, urging Ashe to finish the last mouthful. Goddess! Is that why he'd slumbered where he sat? Had she put in a sleeping draught so Ashe could not save his dog from slaughter? Did she now intend to kill his son, too?

If Death came now, it would be welcome. Oak's friends would not miss him. His family might grieve, but surely not for long? In all honesty, they'd be better off without him. Death would be easier than seeing Horse killed. Knowing he'd betrayed him.

When he felt himself sinking into oblivion, Oak blessed the darkness.

WILLOW

Oak woke thinking he was at home.

His eyes opened, then closed again.

It was night. There should have been nothing but the sounds of breathing, people mumbling in their sleep, snoring, farting, owls hooting, the rustle of mice and voles in the grass, the stink of a hunting fox.

But he could hear talking. Voices, raised in anger. Rowan shouting.

And then his sister. Bending over him, telling him to wake up, trying to pull him into a sitting position. But he was tired; he needed sleep.

Willow slapped him, the flat of her hand hard against his cheek.

He opened his eyes. In the dim light he saw there was a deep cut on her chin. Not fresh, yet not healed either. And all her hair had been cut off. A token of mourning. Goddess! Who had perished? Not their father?"

"Who?" he croaked. "Who died?"

"What?" For a moment Willow looked mystified, then her hand went to her head. "Oh, this? It was a mistake. No one's dead. Not yet." Her face contorted, but not with grief. Oak realized with a jolt of shock that his sister was terrified.

To one side of him there was a low groan and Willow's eyes widened.

"Get up, Oak," she hissed. "Now."

There was a man lying on the ground, his hair spread across the leaf litter. That beak-like nose was familiar, but he was not Deer clan. Something oozed from his head. Blood?

Had Willow hit him? Why?

"We need to go," she whispered. "Come on, Oak! Do I have to carry you?"

Oak's mind was thick with mist, sight and sound were blurred. His sister pulled him to his feet. With her arm around his waist and his over her shoulders, she began half dragging him across the forest floor. Even in his befuddled state Oak knew that something was terribly wrong. They seemed to be in danger. They seemed to be fleeing from someone yet they were leaving a trail of broken branches and disturbed leaf litter that would be easy for even a child to follow.

And there was something else.

Something was missing.

What was it?

Horse!

Oak stopped.

His mind suddenly cleared.

Willow was alive! She was here and she was alive! Oh, thank the Goddess for that! But...

"Horse," he said, turning back. "Horse."

"No," said Willow, pulling him on.

"I can't leave."

"You have to."

"No! I have to get Horse."

He tried to struggle out of her grip but she held him tight.

"It's dead, Oak. They killed it. Come on! Come on!!"

His legs gave way. Willow couldn't hold him and they both sank to the ground.

Horse was dead?

"No..."

Grief and guilt drowned him and he could not contain the long, low moan that oozed from his throat.

But then a scream split the night air. Not human: animal. Horse.

Where are you?

He could feel its white-hot fear, its blazing rage.

I'm coming!

He stared at his sister. "You lied?"

"No ... I heard them! They had knives. They said—"

"But did you see it? Did you *see* it?"

"No," she admitted. "But we can't go back. They want to kill you!"

"I know." He looked at his sister. "How did you find me, Willow?"

"Rowan. After the hunt, Father wanted to set out in search of you. She told him you were drowned; that the Goddess had shown her a vision."

"And so you cut your hair?"

"Of course." Tears began to run down her cheeks. "Father was distraught. He was driven out of his mind with grief. Rowan gave him a sleeping draught to ease his pain. But I couldn't believe you were gone, Oak. I'd know if you weren't alive. I'd feel it, here." She thumped her chest. "I couldn't sleep that night. I went out walking. I spoke your name. I called it over and over. And when your angry spirit didn't come to haunt me, I knew she'd lied. I went to find Rowan but she had gone. There was no time to waste. I tracked her. It was so difficult, it took so long! I did not get here much before they brought you in. I hid. I watched. I waited for my chance. Father will be in agony. Come, Oak. We need to get home."

"No. They killed Fang. I won't let them hurt Horse. I have to go back for him."

"You can't. I won't let you!"

"I must."

"They'll kill you!"

"Better to be dead than live knowing I abandoned Horse."

Willow looked at her brother. He was not the boy he'd been just a few short days ago. She couldn't begin to understand but she could see there was no stopping him.

"Wait. Wait!" She held him still. "Think, Oak. Think. You can't just walk back in there. We need a plan."

There was nothing in Oak's head but desperation.

What would stop the Bears? What would distract them? What would fill their minds, take their attention away from him and Horse? He could think of nothing; it was so hot, so humid, the air so thick and damp. Thunder – distant but distinct – rumbled through the night air. Oak slapped his hand down in frustration. Beneath his palm the forest floor was tinder-dry. The image of a beak-nosed man, his curly hair spread across the leaf litter dropped into his mind.

"The man who was guarding me – the one you knocked out," Oak said suddenly. "Was that your friend Fin?"

"A friend no longer!" Willow said bitterly. She seemed in real, physical pain. "I thought he was a good man, but then I saw him bring my captive brother in. He was lucky I did not kill him!"

"No, no, you're wrong. I mean, you're right – he is a good man. He didn't agree with what they were doing to me."

"But he still did it. He's a Bear, Oak. All Bears are enemies now."

"No. Not him. He's different, I'm sure of it. And he really likes you."

The whites of Willow's eyes were bright in the darkness. "Does he?" She couldn't disguise the sudden hope in her voice.

"Yes. Birra mocked him for it."

"Really?" A smile almost cracked her face apart. "Then maybe he'll help us?"

"It depends how hard you hit him," said Oak, with a grin. "Find him. He could tell the sages I've escaped into the forest. He could lead the Bears off in pursuit. Then I can creep in and cut Horse loose."

It was the thinnest of plans with only the slimmest

chance of success and they both knew it. But with a small laugh, Willow said, "I'll do it." She handed Oak her knife. "You'll need this." She punched his shoulder. "Goddess bring you luck. I'll wait for you at the camp's edge."

"No, you must not. They don't know you're here; they won't come looking for you. Find Fin, then get away," Oak said. "As fast as you can. Leave no trail. Go straight home. Tell our father I'll be back if I can."

"And if not?"

"Tell him I was trying to save a friend."

SACRIFICE

Creep and freeze. Creep. Freeze. Move silently, over twigs that snap, through leaves that rustle and thorns that catch in hair and scratch flesh. Make no sound. Move from shadow to shadow. Avoid those shafts of moonlight that penetrate the canopy.

If Oak had been in full command of his body, it would not have been so difficult. But his feet felt strangely numb, his hands too large, too heavy at the end of his arms.

There were angry voices, rumblings of discontent in the Bear camp, and Oak hoped their noise would cover any mistake he made. But the air was heavy with fear and he knew that fearful people are alert ones. Their attention might be on the sages for now, but if he made a foolish move, they would be on him in an instant.

Horse had already smelled him, heard him. The animal's ears were flicked back in Oak's direction, pointing like arrows indicating the line of his approach.

Horse pulled against the hide ropes that bound it, trying to turn its head so it could catch sight of the boy, nostrils flaring, snorting, breath coming in short gasps, eyes rolling as it felt the ties tighten.

Calm down. I'm coming.

But Horse did not calm down. Oak reached out his thoughts but found only a wall of fury. The animal was coiled, tense, hindquarters bunched, ready to kick out at the slightest provocation.

Getting it loose, even if they were not seen, was going to be harder than he'd thought. Willow's knife was sharp, but the ropes were thick. It would take time to cut through, and with Horse in such a state Oak doubted it would stand still long enough.

Don't think ahead, Oak told himself. *Solve one problem, then the next. Wait for Willow to find Fin. Then snatch whatever chance the Goddess gives.*

He had got as close to Horse as he dared. He could do nothing but wait now. Wait. And listen.

It seemed that a great debate was raging around the fire, and he was the subject of it. The Bear elders were shouting back and forth, arguing about whether

Oak's sacrifice would appease the Goddess or mortally offend her.

"You said the drought was caused by that dog. And yet the thing was killed and the drought continued!" called a beak-nosed man from the crowd. Not Fin, but maybe his kin?

"The Goddess has sent a vision since then," said Rowan. "I have seen what the boy will do. Bending the wild to his will! Attacking his own kind! He must be stopped."

A younger woman's voice: "How can you betray your own clan?"

"I have no choice. The Goddess told me at his birth that the Deer clan's fortunes would rise with him. I thought it was a prophecy that meant only good. But now I see it was her warning. She means me to act. If the Deer people rise, it will be at your expense, and that of all the other clans. It will harm Mother Earth herself. This is for the greater good."

The same woman, incredulous now: "You will slaughter a child? One you yourself delivered into this world? You think murder will not offend the Goddess?"

Alder the seer spoke, his voice deep, resonant. "Not murder. *Sacrifice*. This one life must be taken to preserve the many. The Goddess is already displeased.

Time and time again the Deer people have broken her rules. It is they who have caused this drought. If we do not do this, it will continue. She has storm clouds already gathered in her hand; she is ready to pour water on the earth, but only once this thing is done."

"Enough." Roc got to his feet. He rubbed the scar that ran across his throat. "All have had a chance to speak. We do nothing but go around in circles. Let's finish this." He threw back his head and yelled, "Bring the boy!"

For a moment or two there was no sound but the crackle of flames and the breathing of the gathered Bears who had shuffled back to make way for Oak to be brought into their midst. The moment stretched out. And when no one came, people darted anxious looks towards their chief and let slip murmurs of concern. Roc prepared to shout again, but then there was the sound of feet and Fin came staggering into the midst of his clan, hand clutched to his injured head. Before he could speak, a bolt of lightning tore across the night sky, striking the ancient oak some two paces from where Roc stood. It was ablaze in an instant.

The storm clouds overhead were not yet spilling their load. Fire in a parched forest would spread and spread quickly – faster than a man could run – consuming every living thing in its path. A gust of wind had already fanned the flames, blowing them from the oak to a second tree.

Horse, boy: both were forgotten. Panic swept through the clan. Roc shouted orders, but both his and Alder's voices were drowned as parents screamed for their children. Sleeping sacks, provisions – all were abandoned as families fled. And Fin. Fin was gone, running in the opposite direction to the rest of his clan. Running, Oak hoped, after Willow.

Oak seized his chance. Keeping low to the ground, he ran the short distance across the clearing to where Horse stood trembling. They were both in the path of the fire. Horse smelled it, saw it, and was gripped by a terror beyond any other. This was a predator that could not be kicked or bitten. This was a predator that could not be outrun. It pulled against the ropes, desperate to flee.

The first was so taut that when Oak brought down Willow's knife, the thing snapped, lashing his face and drawing blood.

Horse felt it break and leaped forward, forgetting the second rope, which tightened around its throat, wheeling it in a circle around the tree stump. It kicked out – angry, maddened with pain, blinded by terror.

In the dark and the smoke the animal seemed to

Oak to be in its death throes. He couldn't get past it to the tree stump, to the rope.

Horse was fighting. Fighting him. The enemy.

Hate you, hate you, hate you!

The trees at the edge of the clearing had become a wall of raging red. Oak had to get away before the flames reached him. But not without Horse, never without Horse, no matter how enraged the animal was.

Horse was no longer the listening, inquisitive, trusting creature it had been. It was a whirling, biting, kicking ball of equine fury and as dangerous as any predator.

It reared, striking out at Oak's head with its front hooves.

But the rope snapped it back and it missed.

Oak ducked, rolled, darted under the animal's belly and made for the tree stump. The rope had cut deep into the wood, he couldn't sever it there. When he tried to grab it further up, Horse spun around, whipping the rope away.

But Horse was weakening. The flames were creeping across the floor of the clearing, nearer with each gasping breath.

For just a moment Horse seemed to sag, drawing strength for another outburst.

Oak took his chance and sawed away at the hide, through one more strand, then two.

Shouts came from behind.

Oak had been seen.

In his panic he dropped the knife, scrabbled around in the dirt, found it. Sweat and blood made the hilt slippery in his hands. The blade cut another strand. And another.

Rowan's voice – slicing through the wall of flame: "Get the boy! Kill him!"

Oak slashed so hard that the blade of Willow's precious knife broke.

But the rope was finally severed.

Horse felt the rope slacken as it slid from its throat down its neck to its shoulders. It drew in a breath.

Smoke. Heat. Death.
Run!

Horse didn't wait for Oak to vault on its back – its thoughts were only of flight. As were Oak's. The end of the rope was still in his hands. When he felt Horse gather itself, he leaped, snatching a handful of neck hair, springing upwards and onto its back.

No! Get off me, Thing!

When Horse reared, Oak was thrown back, but his feet locked together around the animal's neck. Clinging to the rope, he stayed in place.

Buck. Buck. Buck!

Still it could not throw the boy.

Scrape Thing off under trees.
Run!

This was not the harmonious, mind-melding gallop by the rolling water, where horse and boy had been so perfectly in tune. This was fear and stink and chaos. This was a fight. Horse wanted rid of him.

The animal could see better and further than Oak could. Though the undergrowth was thick, Horse moved more quickly through it than Oak would have believed possible. He could not see the obstacles all around, but he could feel Horse's temper raging, sense its determination to shed its rider. When Horse swung suddenly to Oak's knife-side, he glimpsed a tree trunk. Horse scraped against it, trying to smash the boy's knee into the bark, but Oak was too quick, throwing himself forward, raising his legs, stretching them along Horse's spine, out of the way. Frustrated, Horse lowered its head, careering towards a low hanging branch that would scrape Oak off. Oak slid to the side.

The wind at their backs blew smoke uphill, chasing the flames after them like a pack of wolves. Oak swung and slid and twisted with each move Horse made, and – though his skin was scraped, though his flesh was bruised – he stayed on Horse's back.

The fire stretched in both directions, a red line bleeding through the forest. It was a barrier between them and the Bear clan, and for that Oak was grateful. But it was driving them further into Bear territory, further away from home and help. Further from Willow.

Flames whipped higher as the wind picked up, spreading the fire wider.

Horse's rage finally subsided. Instinct to survive took over. It was more important to flee than to waste energy ridding himself of the parasite that stuck to his back like a leech.

Horse ran.

FIRE

Boy and horse did not run alone.

The moment Oak had first been led into the forest, he'd noticed how it hummed with life. Beetles crawled underfoot; the air was thick with insects; birds called from the trees. And occasionally he'd heard the tread of something larger through the leaf litter: the crashing of a boar, the light step of a deer, the scrabbling of a squirrel or weasel.

Now the forest creatures were trying to escape the flames. Through the roar of the fire Oak could hear anguished squeals, roars, barks of alarm. He caught brief glimpses of fleeing animals – fox, badger, wolverine. Then, from somewhere behind them, a bird burst from the flames, its tail alight. It flapped over Oak's head, its agonized shrieks piercing his ears, before crashing into a tree and falling to the ground. From the bird's flaming feathers a second fire blazed to life ahead of them, consuming the dry moss that hung from the bark. Horse swung away from it.

Soaked with sweat, which frothed on neck and flanks, crusting white as it dried in the intense heat, how much further could Horse run? And with fire at their backs, fire to one side … how long before they were encircled? How long before their lungs filled with smoke and they could breathe no more? Oak's lips felt as if they were cracking, his throat was parched. Beneath him, Horse wheezed and heaved.

Was it going to end here? Had he thwarted the will of the Goddess by cutting Horse loose? Did she intend for them both to die?

No! It could not be! If that was so, why had she not drowned them in the river?

Oak raised his face to the sky. His mouth was so dry he could not speak. Silently he prayed, *Help us, Goddess. Please.*

And she must have taken pity on him, Oak thought later. Because his plea was answered by a great streak of lightning that cracked the sky in two. A clap of thunder followed, so loud it was as though a mountain had been hurled to the ground. And then the clouds were ripped apart and the Goddess emptied upon the earth the water she had been with-holding for so long.

Raindrops hissed into steam as they met the flames. But more came. More. It cascaded, a river falling from the sky.

Horse came to a stop and Oak slackened the rope, pulling it off as he slid from the animal's back, tying it around his own waist.

He wanted to thank Horse, to rub and scratch his friend the way he liked. But Horse backed away, out of reach.

Oak had saved Horse's life but lost his trust. And that hurt was far deeper than any physical wound.

UNFORGIVEN

Oak was so exhausted he couldn't take another step. There, in the rain, in the charred, ruined forest, Oak slept.

When he woke, he was horrified to see an angry red glow spread across the sky and it took him a moment to realize that it was not fire but sunrise. The rain had stopped for now, but that flaming sky held the promise of more to come. Rain would swell the river and make crossing it back to Deer land even harder. Would Willow be all right? Oak prayed to the Goddess, begging her to protect his sister and see her safely home. Fin, too, if he was with her.

Horse stood a little way off. Like Oak, once the fire was extinguished he had been too tired to move far – but now hunger would propel their legs, thought Oak.

Both needed to find food.

The night before, Horse had not let him near. Hoping that the dawning of a new day might have softened his rage, Oak tried to approach.

The animal did not gallop away. But neither would he let Oak touch him.

Oak knew that Horse didn't know what to do. He hated Oak. *Hated* him. But in this strange, unfamiliar landscape – where everything stank of smoke and ash – Oak was all that was familiar. Horse didn't know where to go or where to find food. Though his head was raised, his nostrils wide, the smell of wet, burned wood and forest creatures was too strong to catch a scent of grass.

Oak edged closer.

Horse ran at Oak, teeth bared, ready to bite.

Oak danced aside. He could feel Horse wanting him to go away, to be left alone. But he couldn't abandon him. Oak tried again, and once more was driven away.

Horse was angry. As angry as the old female had been all that time ago when he had nipped her rump. The matriarch had punished Horse, driving him away from the herd. And he had apologized, head low, licking, chewing.

Horse lifted his head. Whinnied. A long, desperate scream to the herd. *Where are you?*

But no answering call came.

Only Thing, whickering, *I'm here. I'm here.*

Horse glanced at it.

Thing kept its head lowered, its back bent. It chewed noisily, circling him, edging closer. *Sorry. Sorry!*

Humph! Horse could run away. He could move much faster than Thing could on its stumpy, deformed hind legs. But a horse without a herd is easy prey.

Horse would not forget what Thing had done.

Horse would not forgive.

But he might tolerate.

He stood. When Thing came close and pressed his forehead against his shoulder, Horse did not bite.

PURSUIT

They were high on a stretch of forested hillside. The fire had cleared a great swathe of land below them, reducing trees to blackened stumps. The corpses of animals that had not run far or fast enough lay dotted over the ground.

Oak found a hedgehog, choked by smoke, dead and charred but with enough edible flesh to satisfy his hunger. As he chewed, Oak surveyed the changed landscape.

He thought he could see the river in the far distance, glinting through the trees in the sunrise, red as a streak of blood. It was as he'd feared: the fire had driven them further from home.

Home! He so badly wanted to be amongst his own people, to comfort his father, to find out if Willow was safe. But getting there would mean travelling across the scorched earth and back through Bear clan territory. And even if they survived that, how could he persuade Horse to cross the river? It was not possible.

But down over there – to his knife-hand side – another line of fire had cut a broad path that ran to the top of a hill, and through it Oak glimpsed mountains. If he and Horse could reach them, then they could turn in the direction of the setting sun and find the river that way. If they followed far and high enough, it would surely thin to a stream and maybe – if the Goddess willed it – he could persuade Horse to cross.

Oak was wondering how much he could ask of Horse when the animal snorted and stamped his foot.

A warning.

Oak was not fool enough to ignore it a second time.

He looked to where Horse's ears were pointing. At the fringes of the forest way below was movement. Figures emerged from the trees onto the charred hillside.

They were some distance away, picking their way between the ruins of their homeland, but now yelling.

They must have heard Horse's desperate whinny.

Alder and Rowan had not given up.

Oak and Horse had been seen. And now they were being hunted.

. . .

What should Oak do? Rowan had known him all his life – she knew how he thought.

So do the unexpected.

He was not the boy he had been before he met Horse. That boy would have run blindly away.

Reaching the burned path that led towards the mountains meant first heading downhill and nearer to the Bears. Could he and Horse make it before they came within range of their spears?

There was only one way to find out. He swung himself up onto Horse's back.

There, he said.

No!
Danger!
Go! says Thing. Run! Why?
Water? Grass?

Horse sprang forward.

Had the land been flat and clear, Horse could easily have crossed it. But there were fallen trees, charred stumps, holes that could trap a hoof, snap a leg. The animal had to pick his way carefully and Oak could do nothing to guide him. Horse knew the danger they were in as well as Oak did, and he knew the way to go. All Oak could do was sit astride and not impede him.

Horse was moving faster than a running man, but the distance they had to travel was greater than that of the Bears. They could move nothing like fast enough. And now the Bears saw what they planned and were circling round to bar their way.

Some carried spears. Others had fixed arrows to their bowstrings. Oak knew that they were still out of range, but there was one who had broken away from the rest of the pack. One who'd anticipated Horse's route sooner and was closer, much closer than the rest. Very soon he'd be close enough to throw his spear.

Birra.

Oak had nothing but the length of hide rope around his waist. He untied it, and held it in his knife hand.

When Birra hurled his spear, it was with deadly aim, intending to take down Horse. Oak would be much easier to capture if he was on foot.

Scarcely knowing what he did, Oak whipped the rope through the air, catching the spear's blade, flicking it off course. So instead of piercing the flesh of Horse's neck, the blade sliced through thick hair, wedging itself just as Oak's knife had once done. He pulled the spear loose.

Birra was still coming, running with a knife in his hand now. He was within striking distance when Horse stopped, wheeled around and bucked, kicking out at him.

Roc's son ducked and rolled and was up again but Horse swung back around to face him. Oak brandished the spear, raising it high, ready to strike. One downward thrust was all it would take.

There was no need. Birra, unhurt but suddenly terrified by the deadly combination of boy and horse and spear, fell to his knees and crawled away. Horse ran free.

Together, Oak and Horse had speed; they had their combined strength and knowledge.

And now they had a weapon.

Fire had scorched a path up the hill but not down the other side. By midday it was raining steadily, a slow, persistent drizzle that seeped through Oak's tunic and made Horse look as though he'd been immersed in the river. They crested the hill and came to a place where the trees closed about them and they could only move slowly through the thick undergrowth. They pressed on, thirsty, hungry, tired. The canopy was dense and direction was impossible to judge. Horse continued to follow the slope down, and when they reached the bottom, began to climb the next hill. Upwards, upwards. Every so often Horse stopped, lifted his head and sniffed the air. Oak hoped he could smell grass, or maybe even his own herd. There was nothing he could do to guide the animal; he had to trust that Horse would find a way out of the forest.

Sure enough, little by little the canopy thinned, the trees grew further apart, the undergrowth less dense. Eventually there were only stunted trunks and branches that were twisted, contorted by cold and wind. And then at last they were beyond the treeline, out on a mountainside in the clear air where there was grass to eat and a stream from which to drink.

They stopped to rest. Horse grazed. Oak knew that if the Bears were pursuing, he and Horse would be easy enough to track.

Would they follow? The drizzle showed no sign of stopping. It was, Oak thought, what the elders would have said was the right kind of rain. Mother Earth would drink deep; trees and grass would grow; fruit would swell. The drought had truly broken even though there had been no sacrifice. Oak hoped the Bears would be satisfied but feared they would not. They had tried to kill him, and the killing of a child violated every clan taboo. Roc would not want Oak telling his tale at the next midsummer gathering and didn't know that Willow had seen and heard every-thing. To Roc's mind the only way of preventing the story from getting out would be to silence Oak. It was best to assume that he and Horse were in danger until they were back on Deer clan land.

MOUNTAIN

Hunting took time. Grazing took time. Resting, sleeping, picking their way across rocky terrain that was utterly unknown to Oak all took time.

And the Bears were not giving up.

The very next day, when he and Horse were high on the exposed mountainside, Oak saw them below, a line of dots emerging from the treeline. Dogged. Determined. Relentless. They would keep on coming, grinding their prey to exhaustion, waiting for the moment to strike.

Had Oak known the lie of this land, Horse's speed would have made their pursuers easy to evade. But once, twice, many times they rode in the direction Oak hoped was homeward only to find they had to turn around. They moved across a slope that started gently enough but then turned into scree and Horse could not keep his footing. They passed through a shaded trough between two peaks, which ended in a wall of rock so steep that Horse could not climb it. They waded through a stream that turned into a bog which threatened to suck them both under.

For the length of that first day horse and boy seemed to go in circles. On the next, they climbed higher and the air cooled, the grass became sparse. On the third they found the river at last. They were high above the place where he and Horse had fallen in, Oak thought, but it was still too wide, too fast-flowing for them to cross. Oak hoped they were escaping but feared they were being slowly driven into a trap.

Higher. They had to go higher. The river must surely thin to a stream up there?

The Bears did not catch up with them. But they didn't go home, either.

There were clearly those among them who could hunt, as the smell of roasted meat drifted through the night air to Oak, making his stomach ache with hunger. He had no fire-stones. No cloak. He and Horse slept side by side for warmth, but up here the night air pinched and gave them little rest. He had a spear but the Goddess sent nothing across his path that he could kill. All he could manage to eat were a few snatched berries. A handful of nuts. A root, tugged from the soil. He was eating like a bird, without the advantage of a bird's wings. As for Horse? He was growing leaner too. Weaker.

Shortly after dawn on the fourth morning, Horse and Oak were zigzagging their way up the side of a mountain that grew increasingly sheer. After some time they found themselves on a wide ledge that thinned little by little, until – at around midday – it was so narrow Oak's knee was grazing the wall of rock on his knife-hand side. On his heart side was the river, much thinner now but plummeting through a gaping chasm, its rushing noise magnified by echoes. And then – faintly at first but growing louder with each step – Oak heard something even more unnerving. A groaning, creaking sound, unearthly yet peculiarly human. If it had not been for the volume, Oak would have thought someone very old, with aching joints, was trying to stand up after a long time sitting on hard ground.

They drew nearer to the source of the sound, skirting a jutting outcrop of rock, turning almost back on themselves once, then twice. And there they discovered that the ledge they had been following ran up to the edge of the chasm and went no further. The chasm itself ended in a sheer wall of creaking ice from which a gushing stream of meltwater poured.

They had reached the source of the river, Oak realized. Though he could not see it from beneath, he imagined this was the edge of a lake of frozen water pooled between mountain peaks. He had found the river's end at the rolling water, and now he had found its beginning.

The knowledge was little consolation. Oak's worst fears had come true. Whether by accident or cunning the Bears had him trapped. The only way out was back the way he and Horse had come. And their pursuers were behind them, coming along the ledge fast now, drawing closer, anticipating victory. There was nowhere to run.

Unless...

Oak slid off Horse's back. He walked the few paces to the edge of the chasm. If they could only get across it, they would be free. But it was impossible! The gap was wider than the length of a full-grown man – and several times as deep.

Yet Horse had jumped clean over an aurochs when he'd had to. Could Oak ask him to leap this?

He could hear the Bears calling to each other. Their blood was up, they knew the end was in sight. He climbed back onto Horse.

Jump! he urged. Horse snorted in alarm.

No!

Yet Horse could smell the predators on the wind, getting closer.

Run? Jump?

Horse gathered himself, bounding forward one, two paces. But his heart screamed, *Wrong, wrong, wrong! Galloping water. Dark. Dark.*

Stop!

Hoof hitting stone, slipping, sliding, Horse came to a dead halt at the chasm's edge.

Oak, who'd been hunched over his shoulders, *driving* Horse forward, hanging on to his neck hair as though he could lift the creature over the ravine, was hurled over his ears.

One hand grasped nothing but empty air. The other clung tight to Horse. Oak dangled, feet thrashing. The terrified animal was thrown off balance, the weight of Oak tugging him forward.

No! No!

With the last of his strength, Horse tipped onto his haunches, wheeling away from the chasm and back along the ledge, pulling Oak onto solid ground.

The boy lay there, flat on the rock, trying to catch

his breath. He could hear the sound of the Bears' running feet coming closer. They were moving in for the kill. He had the spear but could not fight so many!

Horse was exhausted. Weak with hunger, addled with fear.

The animal had no faith in him, Oak thought. And he was right. He hadn't been able to save Horse and now they were both going to die.

His father's voice. *The Goddess has given you a brain. Use it.*

Willow, echoing Ashe. *Think, Oak. Think.*

And then Lark's bitter words: *You can lead. But whether we'll follow is up to us.*

Ashe never ordered someone to do what he was not prepared to do himself. Oak had lost Horse's trust, but perhaps there was a way to regain it. If he proved himself worthy, if he led, might Horse follow?

He had to jump first – and he had to jump alone.

Oak gulped down the terror that threatened to overwhelm him. Yes, he might die. But better to fall, better to be smashed to pieces or drown, than have his skull caved in by a Bear's sacrificial axe.

Horse had backed away from the ravine's edge. Oak now pushed him a little further along the ledge to give himself room. He rubbed Horse's neck, kissed his nose.

And then Oak turned to face the chasm. He laid

down the spear, for it would only impede him. He prayed to the Goddess, not to save himself but to protect Horse and see him safely home. Taking a deep breath, he summoned up every morsel of courage he possessed. And then he ran.

Leaped.

And a fraction of a heartbeat later knew that he had not jumped high or hard enough. He was going to fall.

But then he had the strangest sensation. It was as though the air below him gathered itself into a mighty hand. Something brushed his belly, like gigantic fingers nudging him upwards and forwards, holding him in the air for just long enough.

He crashed flat on his face on the other side, cracking his chin, catching his tongue between his teeth. Blood filled his mouth and the air was punched out of him. He lay, gasping for breath like a fish plucked out of water. A horrible, groaning croak came from chest and throat.

He didn't dare look back. It would have been natural – instinctive – for him to turn, to beg Horse to come. But staring into his eyes would scare the animal. Staring into his eyes would make Horse doubt him.

Lead. Lead. Lead and herd will follow.

I know what I'm doing. Trust me. Follow!

Oak climbed shakily to his feet and walked away from the edge.

He felt Horse hesitate. Heard his squeal of panic. And then ...

... a thunder of hooves, a clatter of stones, a rushing of air.

Horse jumped ...

... and landed, muscle and heat and sweat, almost knocking Oak off his feet. He flung his arms around the animal's neck and thanked the Goddess through his tears.

Then he was on Horse's back and the pair were running away from the dreadful ravine. Though Oak could hear the Bears' furious shouts as they rounded the last corner, though he could hear the grunts of effort as they hurled their spears across the chasm, he and Horse were out of range. The weapons clattered and broke on bare rock.

HOMEWARD

The river would guide him home, Oak thought, but he did not want to stick too close to it. Though the Bears had lost their spears, they had knives and arrows. By now they would be desperate, and it was not beyond the bounds of possibility that they would risk trespassing on Deer land to prevent him reaching home. And so he kept it barely within sight, a ribbon of flashing light that twisted and curled through rocks. They slept that night on stony ground in a landscape unfamiliar to Oak. The next day, though, he began to recognize the shape of the mountains. That one over there – he was seeing it from the back, but surely that peak marked the edge of the pass they travelled through on the way to the clan gathering. And that ridge there looked like the one that fringed the mountain lake.

It took a whole day to arrive at the first peak, and to find their way around its vast, sheer mass down into the pass and then along it to the lake. It was sunset when they reached the water. The ridge above it glowed amber and pink; the lake was not sky blue but fiery scarlet.

Remembering how he'd tricked Lark and Yew into jumping in that time, he felt ashamed. He hadn't deserved their friendship, he thought. But things would be different from now on.

"Nearly home," Oak told Horse as he waded in and drank deeply. "I wonder what my father will make of you..."

It was so calm, so peaceful, and they were so very nearly home that Oak relaxed. He began to imagine their faces when they saw him coming over the plateau. Willow must surely have made it back safely? He would know in his guts if she hadn't. If Fin was with her, Oak would have to apologize for throwing that stone at the clan meet...

Suddenly Horse's head shot up. His nostrils flared.

Oak's stomach contracted. Had the Bears followed them? Was this blood-red water an omen, a warning from the Goddess?

Danger?

Horse did not reply but a tremor rippled through

the animal's body. Every muscle was tense, his ears were pricked forward, straining to catch ... what?

Oak could smell nothing, hear nothing. But his senses were so blunt compared to Horse's.

Predator? Wolf? Bear?

No answer.

Horse was wading out of the lake, head up, sniffing the air. He didn't seem afraid. He was excited, Oak realized. Trembling with anticipation, not fear.

Horse's screaming whinny was so loud it hurt Oak's ears. His whole body shook with it.

And then came a faint, distant reply.

Horse was slithering, scrambling down a scree slope towards the plateau and Oak could do nothing but stay on his back and hope not to unbalance him. The animal seemed barely aware of his presence.

It was only when they saw the herd – when the old female trotted towards them and stopped dead at the sight of the boy on Horse's back – that Oak felt the animal reach out to him.

An ear flicked back.

A question.

Oak felt his confusion. Suddenly Horse was not sure what to do. He didn't know where he belonged. With the herd? With him?

He wondered later if he could have *made* Horse

abandon his own kind and come with him. But at the time there seemed to be no question at all about what he should do.

It was the hardest task he'd ever had. Somewhere deep inside himself Oak felt something shatter. But he slid from Horse's back and gave his neck a scratch. Horse did not scratch him back: his attention was on the others.

Oak took a step away and the animal finally turned towards him. He butted him gently and they pressed their foreheads together for one last time.

Then Oak thought, *Go. Go.*

Horse did not need telling. He was off. And Oak had to bite his lip to stop himself crying out, calling after him, begging him not to leave.

He watched Horse join the herd. Saw the sniffing of nostrils. Heard the squeals of excitement, the whickers of recognition. And then many more horses than the fingers on both hands and toes on both feet were kicking up their heels and running for pure joy. Running far, running out of sight, leaving Oak standing with so many tears streaming down his face that he could no longer see.

Walking was strange after being part of Horse for so long. Oak felt reduced to nothing. His legs were stumps, his arms were twigs, his hands were clubs that dangled uselessly at the end of his arms. He was so slow.

But he walked because there was nothing else he could do. He walked even when the sun had disappeared. He knew the way now: the land was calling him home. The ground was hard, the night sky vast. He was exhausted but still he walked.

And then at dawn he saw the smoke rising in the early light. He heard the sounds of people stirring and smelled cooking fires and food and his broken heart mended a little as he limped towards his clan.

FORETELLING

Afterwards, when Oak recalled his homecoming, there were few things he could remember with perfect clarity. One was seeing Willow emerge from their hut yawning. She was carrying a cooking vessel full of liquid but when she caught sight of Oak, she dropped it and shrieked so loudly a flock of birds took flight. Then she was running across the grass towards him, all the while shouting. Shouting for their father and then another name. "Fin! Fin! Fin! He's home! He's safe! He's home!" She swept Oak off his feet, holding him in such a tight embrace he could barely breathe.

"Thank the Goddess!" Fin must have followed close on her heels and soon he was greeting Oak as warmly as if he was his own blood brother.

The second thing Oak remembered clearly was

the shock of seeing his father. The Deer chief had seemed to age years with each day his son had been missing. The long ropes of hair that had once hung down to his hips had been cut in mourning when he'd thought his son dead. The fuzz that remained had turned white as the winter snows with the shock of his daughter's disappearance. He walked stiffly, slowly, like an old man. But that smile! Its brightness would have shamed the sun.

Thereafter the clan had come from their huts to gaze at him. The memory was nothing but a bright blur, one dear, familiar face smudging into another as he was clasped to the chests of each and every elder while children gawped and pointed. He'd grown so used to being alone with Horse that the noise of their voices raised in joyful thanks to the Goddess sounded loud as thunderclaps.

It took a moment for Oak to recognize Lark for her dandelion orb of hair had all been cut off in mourning for him even though she was not blood family. And what little there had been of Yew's had been cropped right back to the scalp. The sight moved Oak more than he could say. He couldn't recall later whether he'd been first to speak or whether it had been one of them. All Oak knew was that one moment they were awkward and shy with each other and the next they were laughing and punching arms and wrestling like puppies.

But it wasn't long before the relief of being home turned to exhaustion. When Ashe saw Oak sag under the weight of the endless questions, he raised his voice and told the clan: "My son is in need of rest. Come back to the hut, Oak. Eat. Sleep. Tonight we will feast. We will hear his story then."

They ate deer meat roasted with juniper and thyme; cakes, made from the corn Ashe had planted and harvested, dripping with honey. Never had anything tasted so good. When Oak was full to bursting, Ashe asked him to address the clan.

He was the chief's son: loyalty to Ashe meant they were duty-bound to listen. But before he started, Oak noticed a few knowing smiles, a few sideways glances and rolled eyes. They expected him to boast, to embellish the truth, to make it all about himself and his own prowess. But those days had gone; he would give them none of that. He was surprisingly nervous and hesitant when he began to speak. He kept his eyes down, his voice low. Though his tale was sensational, he listed only the barest of facts and the more quietly he spoke, the harder they listened. He told them how afraid he'd been, how hard he'd found it to achieve the simplest of tasks, like lighting a fire. He confessed his failings and – though there were astonished gasps and mutterings of amazement when he spoke of riding Horse across the shingle for the first time – he hurried over his achievements. He was interrupted sometimes by questions. As he gave his answers, Oak felt a shift in the clan's attitude towards him. The more humility he showed, the more he seemed to be respected. He was grateful for it and a little overawed.

He did not tell his story alone, for he knew only one half of it. They had held their tongues until he was safely home, but now Willow and then Fin answered the questions that Oak could not.

"Alder has long spoken of a vision from the Goddess," Fin told them. "Many, many moons ago she told him that someone was coming who would bend the wild to his will. In doing so, he would shift the path of all humankind. For good or ill, she did not say. Alder called that person the Changer." He turned to Ashe. "At the clan gathering – long ago – when you first talked of settling in one place, of building huts, Alder began to wonder if it was you. Then you talked of clearing land and planting seeds and he liked that even less.

"When the drought came, he was certain that the Goddess was angered, and he said that the visions had all been warnings: that he was meant to act, to stop these things happening. Then you came to the sacred temple with a dog trotting at your heels, and he was finally convinced you were indeed the Changer. I don't know what he said to Rowan, and I didn't see what he did at the feast. I wasn't there…" Fin glanced at Willow and she slid her hand into his. "It was only when I saw Roc's injuries that I realized what had been done to the dog.

The next day – after you'd left – Alder declared it was the end of the matter. It rained, if you recall, and he was triumphant, but not for long. We returned to the forest and his mood grew darker and darker. And then Rowan came and said she had been sent a vision. The cause of the drought was not the Deer chief, but his son. She had misunderstood the prophecy given at his birth, she said. It was not the promise of a glorious future, but the warning of an evil that must be averted. The boy would lead his people astray, she said. Rowan and Alder were convinced that their two visions aligned and that the Changer must be stopped at all costs. We were sent in search of Oak," he said, head down, unable to meet anyone's eyes. "I was given no choice."

There was a murmuring of disquiet that Ashe quelled in an instant.

"This was not Fin's doing. Our own sage brought this about. Rowan is to blame. It is hard, I know. We trusted her and she turned against us. She has a place in all our hearts – she brought my own children into this world and eased the passing of my wife. And for that I bowed to her wisdom. We all mourn for what she once was to us. We all grieve, and it is right we do so. But there is no shame or blame on Fin," the chief insisted. "When the chance came, he was ready to help us. He is Deer clan now, and most welcome."

Fin smiled, but Oak saw sadness in his eyes. He knew what it was to be without family. "You have paid a high price," Oak said quietly. "I thank you for it."

Fin lowered his head for a moment, but then raised it suddenly and grinned at Willow. "The price was worth paying," he declared.

Ashe addressed the clan. "It will come as no surprise to anyone here that Fin and Willow wish to be handfasted. They have my blessing. Does anyone here object?"

His question was met by silence.

"Good," said Ashe. "Well then, the ceremony will take place as soon as we can find a new sage."

Any tension there had been found its release in the laughter that rippled around the gathering. The story was ended. Only one question remained: what had the Goddess shown Rowan on the cave wall that had frightened her so badly she'd betrayed her own people?

To enter the sacred cave had been forbidden, yet now there was no sage to prevent it. And so, the morning after his son's homecoming, Ashe lit a lamp and together he and Oak went into the mountain.

Marking the walls with red clay so they would find their way out more easily, Ashe tracked Rowan's route through the tunnels. A footprint here, a tuft of fur caught on a rock there, a hair, a feather, showed Ashe the way as clearly as if the sage had been leading them. At last they came to the sacred cave.

Ashe was as awed by the drawings that marked the walls as Oak had been that first time. And now, Oak thought, on his second visit, they were no less astounding. There was a mighty power here that he could not begin to comprehend. His eyes roamed the walls. He looked once more at the picture of the hunt. There he was, drawn with his arms raised: not making a kill but making what had seemed at the time to be a most disastrous mistake.

Together, father and son crossed the cave floor. There in the corner, depicted clearly with a few sweeps of charcoal, was a boy on the back of a horse.

He held a spear above his head and was pointing it at a man who cowered below him.

"Birra," said Oak. Birra, son of Roc, in the charred stumps of the forest. Birra, who'd been unhurt but had crawled away in abject terror.

The Goddess had shown the scene. But Rowan had misread it.

"I wasn't attacking," Oak told Ashe. "I was defending myself. And Horse."

"I know it," said Ashe gently.

"I don't understand." Oak ran his fingers over the lines on the cave wall, smudging them. "I'd never have done that if she hadn't gone to the Bears. If they hadn't come looking for me, I'd have followed the river home. They were camped a long way away from it – our paths wouldn't even have crossed. If Birra hadn't thrown his spear, I'd never have threatened him. By trying to stop it happening, Rowan made sure it did!"

Alone with his father in the sacred cave Oak shared something he had not mentioned at the feast.

"I said I jumped the chasm, and I did. But I was going to fall, I know I was. And then ... something stopped me. Held me up. Just for a moment. Was it the wind? I might have been imagining things. It felt like the hand of the Goddess. Does that sound stupid?"

"No. It sounds strange, but not stupid. Oak, I can no

more explain these things than you. These visions the sages have seen … are they a warning? Or a promise? Are these things we are meant to prevent? Or things we are meant to do? Who can say?"

Oak asked, "What about the rest of it? Us, rising above the other clans? Will they try and stop it happening? This isn't the end, is it?"

"We will see. The seasons will turn, the next clan gathering will come. Until then? Rest. Eat. Enjoy the fellowship of your people. None of us – not even the wisest sage – can know all the future. But we have learned one thing for certain: that signs, however clear they seem, are easily misinterpreted." Ashe rested a hand on his son's shoulder. "We were given brains to think and we must use them. And yet a human mind is such a small thing compared to that of the divine. We cannot ever understand everything. No one person can know what truly lies in the heart of the Goddess." He smiled sadly. "In future I will distrust anyone who tells me they do."

THE BEGINNING

Horse had come back to his herd. Standing in their midst sniffing noses with Old Mare, he breathed in the pictures from her mind: he saw the stallion, killed by a lynx, heard his screams, smelled his blood.

The herd was without a leader.

Old Mare felt the difference in him. He was no longer the upstart colt who'd been washed away in Galloping Water. He had been gone less than a moon's waning, but he was older, wiser.

And there was something new. Something different. He had a knowledge that she did not; a power that she knew nothing of.

She lowered her head; yielded to him.

He was Leader.

And so while they slept, he stayed awake, watching over the herd.

Responsibility was a weight on his back, like carrying Thing. It was not heavy, but he had to adjust his bearing. He listened to the distant howl of wolves and remembered the ones that had snapped at his heels, that had come so close to bringing him down. Until Thing saw them off with his flying claw.

Thing had saved them both.

He was Horse. But he was something more too. At dawn some instinct nudged him in Thing's direction.

And because Horse was Leader, his herd followed.

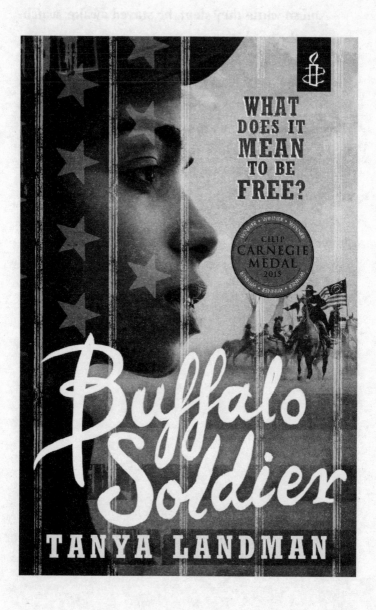

WHAT
DOES IT
MEAN
TO BE
FREE?

WINNER · WINNER · WINNER
CILIP
CARNEGIE
MEDAL
2015
WINNER · WINNER · WINNER

*Buffalo
Soldier*

TANYA LANDMAN

Buffalo Soldier

Winner of the CILIP Carnegie Medal

What kind of girl steals the clothes from a dead man's
back and runs off to join the army?
A desperate one that's who.

World been turned on its head by that big old war,
and the army seemed like the safest place to be,
until we was sent off to fight them Indians. And then?
Heck! When Death's so close you can smell his breath,
ain't nothing makes you feel more alive.

––––––•–•–––––

"Gripping, vivid, superb."
Independent

"Deeply thrilling … a must-read."
Amnesty International

"Hard-hitting, bleak and full of heart."
Metro

I WILL
LIVE
& I WILL
FIGHT
FOR I AM A
WARRIOR

APACHE

TANYA LANDMAN

CARNEGIE MEDAL-WINNING AUTHOR

Apache

Shortlisted for the CILIP Carnegie Medal

I was in my fourteenth summer when the Mexicans rode against us. Twelve moons later, I took my revenge. And though Ussen has drawn visions of a terrible future in my mind, I will not be vanquished. I belong to this land: to the wide sky above my head, to the sweet grass beneath my feet. Here must I die.

But first I will live, and I will fight. For I am a warrior.

I am Apache.

———◆———

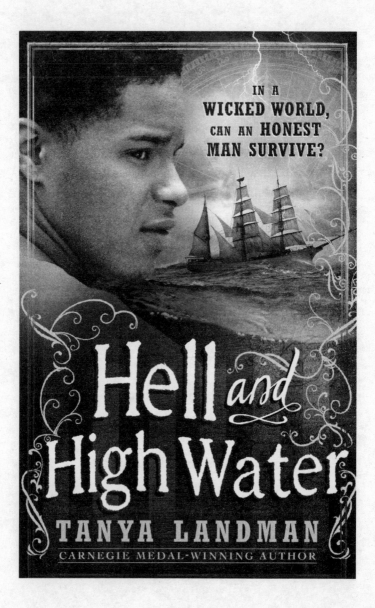

IN A
WICKED WORLD,
CAN AN HONEST
MAN SURVIVE?

Hell and High Water

TANYA LANDMAN

CARNEGIE MEDAL-WINNING AUTHOR

Hell and High Water

Shortlisted for the *Guardian* Children's Fiction Prize

It was a man. Drowned. Dead.

Lying on the sand, waves breaking over his back.

The body should be moved, but Caleb couldn't manage it alone.

Yet who in this godforsaken place would help him?

When his father is arrested and transported to the Colonies, Caleb is left alone. After a desperate journey in search of an aunt he's never met he receives a strange, cold welcome. Then a body washes up on the nearby beach and Caleb is caught up in a terrifying net of lies and intrigue. Soon he and his new family are in mortal danger.

———◆———

"Beautifully written and wonderfully paced."
Guardian

"Gripping … Landman's research is impeccable."
The Times

"An amazing novel which left me lost for words – everyone should read it. Can I give it eleven out of ten?"
Guardian Children's Book Website

TANYA LANDMAN is the author of many books for children and young adults. She is best known for her award-winning historical novels for teenagers, including *Buffalo Soldier*, which won the Carnegie Medal and *Apache*, which was shortlisted for the Carnegie Medal and the Booktrust Teenage Fiction Prize, and also *The Goldsmith's Daughter*, *Hell and High Water* and *Beyond the Wall*. For *Mondays are Murder*, the first in her hugely popular middle-grade murder mystery series, she won the Red House Children's Book Award, which was voted for entirely by children. You can find out more about Tanya and her books by visiting her website: www.tanyalandman.com